MARRIED BY CHRISTMAS

For better or worse, she'll be his by Christmas!

As the festive season approaches, these darkly handsome Mediterranean men are looking forward to unwrapping their brand-new brides. Whether they're living luxuriously in London or flying by private jet to their glamorous European villas, these arrogant, commanding tycoons need wives, and they'll have them—by Christmas!

Don't miss any of the exciting stories available this month from Harlequin Presents EXTRA:

Hired: The Italian's Convenient Mistress
by Carol Marinelli

The Spanish Billionaire's Christmas Bride
by Maggie Cox

Claimed for the Italian's Revenge
by Natalie Rivers

The Prince's Arranged Bride
by Susan Stephens

SUSAN STEPHENS was a professional singer before meeting her husband on the tiny Mediterranean island of Malta. In true Harlequin Presents style they met on Monday, became engaged on Friday and were married three months later. Almost thirty years and three children later they are still in love. (Susan does not advise her children to return home one day with a similar story as she may not take the news with the same fortitude as her own mother!)

Susan had written several nonfiction books when fate took a hand. At a charity costume ball there was an after-dinner auction. One of the lots, "Spend a Day with an Author," had been donated by Mills & Boon author Penny Jordan. Susan's husband bought this lot and Penny was to become not just a great friend, but a wonderful mentor who encouraged Susan to write romance.

Susan loves her family, her pets, her friends and her writing. She enjoys entertaining, travel and going to the theater. She reads, cooks and plays the piano to relax, and can occasionally be found throwing herself off mountains on a pair of skis or galloping through the countryside.

Visit Susan's Web site, www.susanstephens.net. She loves to hear from her readers all around the world!

THE PRINCE'S ARRANGED BRIDE
SUSAN STEPHENS

~ MARRIED BY CHRISTMAS ~

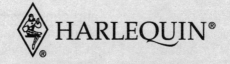

TORONTO • NEW YORK • LONDON
AMSTERDAM • PARIS • SYDNEY • HAMBURG
STOCKHOLM • ATHENS • TOKYO • MILAN • MADRID
PRAGUE • WARSAW • BUDAPEST • AUCKLAND

ISBN-13: 978-0-373-82378-9
ISBN-10:   0-373-82378-9

THE PRINCE'S ARRANGED BRIDE

First North American Publication 2008.

Previously published in the U.K. under the title
THE ITALIAN PRINCE'S PROPOSAL.

Copyright © 2003 by Susan Stephens.

www.eHarlequin.com

Printed in U.S.A.

THE PRINCE'S
ARRANGED BRIDE

For Steve, my hero

CHAPTER ONE

CROWN PRINCE ALESSANDRO BUSSONI OF FERARA narrowed amber eyes in lazy speculation as he continued to stare at the brightly lit stage. 'She'd do.'

'I beg your pardon, sir?'

There was no emotion in the question. The man sitting next to the Prince on the top table at the lavish Midsummer ball wore the carefully controlled expression of a career diplomat, and had a voice to match. Thin and lugubrious, with sun-starved features, it would have been impossible for Marco Romagnoli to provide a sharper contrast to his employer, and Crown Prince Alessandro's blistering good looks were supported by one of the brightest minds in Europe, as well as all the presence and easy charm that was his by right of birth.

'I said she'd do,' the Prince repeated impatiently, turning a compelling gaze on his aide-de-camp. 'You've paraded every woman of marriageable age before me, Marco, and failed to tempt me once. I like the look of this girl—'

And it was a lot more than just her stunning appearance, Alessandro acknowledged silently as his glance went back to the stage. The girl possessed an incredible energy not dissimilar to his own—an energy that seemed to leap out from the gaudily dressed performance area and thump him straight in the chest.

All he had to offer her was a cold-blooded business deal,

but… His sensuous mouth curved in a thoughtful smile. In this instance mixing business with pleasure might not be such a bad thing.

'Are you serious, Your Royal Highness?' Marco Romagnoli murmured, taking care not to alert their fellow diners.

'Would I joke about so serious a matter as my future wife? Alessandro demanded in a fierce whisper. 'She looks like fun.'

'Fun, sir?' Marco Romagnoli leaned forward to follow his employer's eyeline. 'You are talking about the singer with the band?'

'You find something wrong with that?' the Prince demanded, swivelling round to level a challenging gaze on his aide's face.

'No, sir,' Marco returned in a monotone, knowing the Prince would brook no prejudice based on flimsy face-value evidence. 'But if I may ask an impertinent question…?'

'Ask away,' Alessandro encouraged, his firm mouth showing the first hint of amusement as he guessed the way Marco's mind was working.

'She'd do for what, exactly, sir…? Only she's rather—'

'Luscious? Bold? Striking? In your face? What?' the Prince prompted adjusting his long legs as if the enforced in-activity was starting to irk him.

'All of those,' Marco suggested uncomfortably, his glance flashing back to the stage, where Emily Weston was well into her third number and clearly had the affluent, well-oiled crowd eating out of her hand. 'I can see that a young lady like that holds a certain attraction for—' Marco Romagnoli eased his fingers under a starched white collar that seemed to be on the point of choking him.

'Go on. Don't stop now,' Prince Alessandro encouraged, reining in his amusement.

Taking a few moments to rethink his approach, the usually unflappable courtier replied carefully, 'Well, sir, I can see she's a beauty, and undoubtedly perfect for certain activities. But you surely can't be thinking—'

'You mean I should bed her, not wed her?' Alessandro suggested dryly, as he looked back to where Emily had the microphone clutched between both hands for a slow number, looking as if she was about to devour it.

'I couldn't have put it better myself, sir. In my opinion such an ill-judged match would only create more problems than it would solve.'

'I disagree,' the Crown Prince of Ferara countered, 'and nothing you can say will persuade me that the girls you have paraded before me would fill the role any better—or vacate it without causing problems.'

He paused, and took another long look at the stage. 'As it is not my intention to break any hearts, Marco, this is the perfect solution. I want a straightforward business deal and a short-term bride—'

'Short-term, sir?'

Alessandro turned to answer the disquiet so clearly painted across the other man's face.

'I know,' he said, leaning closer to ensure they were not overheard. 'You're thinking of all the other implications such an arrangement would entail—I would expect nothing less of you, my old friend.'

The Prince's companion grew ever more troubled. Even if he could have shed the role of cautious professional advisor, Marco Romagnoli had known Alessandro from the day of his birth, and was considered an honorary member of the royal family.

'I wouldn't wish to see anyone take advantage of you, sir,' he said now, with concern.

'I shall take good care to ensure that none of the parties involved in my plan is taken advantage of,' Alessandro assured him. 'Thanks to our country's archaic legislation I can think of no other way to solve the problem of succession.

If my father is to have his wish and retire I must marry immediately. It's obvious to me that this young woman has spirit. When I put my proposition to her I think she will have an instant grasp of the advantages that such a match can bring to both of us.'

'Yes, sir,' Marco agreed reluctantly, flinching visibly as Emily launched into a raunchy upbeat number.

'I have seen enough, Marco,' the Prince said, reclaiming his aide's attention. 'And I like what I see. Please advise the young lady that Alessandro Bussoni wishes to talk with her after the performance tonight. No titles,' he warned. 'And if she asks, just say I have a proposition to put to her. And don't forget to ask her name,' he added as, without another word, Marco Romagnoli rose to his feet.

After the show, Emily Weston, the singer with the band, was having a tense debate over the phone with her twin sister Miranda.

'Well, how *do* you deal with them?' she demanded, shouldering the receiver to scoop up another huge blob of cleansing cream from her twin's industrial-sized pot.

'Who do you mean?' Miranda snuffled between ear-splitting sneezes.

'Stage Door Johnnies—'

Miranda's summer cold symptoms dissolved into laughter. 'Stage Door Whosies?'

'Don't pretend you don't know what I'm talking about,' Emily insisted, flashing another concerned glance towards the dressing room door.

'I didn't think there was such a thing as Stage Door Johnnies nowadays,' Miranda said doubtfully.

'Well, I can assure you there is,' Emily insisted. 'What else would you call uninvited gentleman callers who won't take no for an answer?'

'Depends on who's doing the calling, I suppose,' Miranda

conceded, blasting out another sneeze. 'Why don't you just take a look at him first, before you decide?'

'No way! That's never been part of our agreement.'

'But if he looks like Herman Munster you can send him packing…and if he's a babe, pass him on to me. He'd never know the difference. If Mum and Dad can't tell us apart, what chance does this man stand? What have you got to lose?'

'Look, I'll have to go,' Emily said as another rap, far more insistent than the last, bounced off the walls around her head. 'I told his messenger I couldn't see anyone I didn't know immediately after a show—pleading artistic temperament. He still hasn't taken the hint.'

'He sent someone round first?' Miranda cut in, her voice taut with excitement. 'He sounds interesting. He might be a VIP.'

'I doubt it,' Emily said as she peered into the mirror to peel off her false eyelashes. 'Though when I said I wouldn't see him I thought his representative muttered something about Prince being disappointed—'

'Emily, you dope,' Miranda exclaimed through another bout of sneezing. 'Prince Records is the recording company my band's been hoping to sign with. And you've just turned away their scout.'

'Can't I get one of the boys to see him?' Emily suggested hopefully. After all, there were five male members in Miranda's band.

'Are you kidding?' Miranda exclaimed. 'First of all they'll be in the pub by now…and secondly, do you seriously think I'd trust them to discuss business without my being there?'

Remembering the dreamy idealism of Miranda's fellow musicians, Emily could only respond in the negative. 'It might have helped if you had warned me this might happen,' she protested reasonably. 'Have to go,' she finished in a rush, wiping her hands on the towel across her lap as another flurry of raps hit the door. 'Whoever this is, he's not about to give up.'

Cutting the connection, Emily grabbed a handful of tissues as she shot up from her seat in front of the brilliantly lit mirror. Then, scooting behind a conveniently placed screen, she called out, 'Come in.'

This was the craziest thing she had ever done, Emily thought nervously as she swiped off the last of her make-up and stuffed the used tissues into the pocket of her robe. She tensed as the door swung open.

'Hello? Miss Weston? Miss Weston, are you there?'

She had heard male voices likened to anything from gravel to bitter chocolate, but this one slammed straight into her senses. Italian, she guessed, and with just the hint of a sexy mid-Atlantic drawl. She pictured him scanning the cluttered space, hunting for her hiding place, and felt her whole being responding to some imperative and extremely erotic wake-up call.

'Make yourself comfortable,' she sang out, relieved she was hidden away. 'I'm getting changed.'

'Thank you, Miss Weston,' the voice replied evenly. 'Please don't hurry on my account.'

Just the authority in the man's voice made the hairs stand on the back of her neck. And there was a stillness about it that made her think of a jungle cat, lithe, impossibly strong—and deadly.

It was in her nature to confront threats, not hide from them. So why was she skulking behind a screen? Emily asked herself impatiently. Could it be that the force of this man's personality had taken possession of what, in Miranda's absence, was her territory?

'Can I help you?' she said, struggling to see through a tiny crack in the woodwork.

'I certainly hope so.'

There was supreme confidence and not a little amusement

in the response, as well as the type of worldliness that had Emily mentally rocking back on her heels. It was almost as if the man had caught her out doing something wrong—as if she had no right to be looking at him.

Drawing a few steadying breaths, she tried again. But all she could see through the crack in the screen was the broad sweep of shoulders clad in a black dinner jacket and a cream silk evening scarf slung casually around the neck of an impressively tall individual. A man whose luxuriant, dark wavy hair was immaculately groomed and glossy…the type of hair that made you want to run your fingers through it and then move on to caress— She pulled herself up short, closing her eyes to gather her senses…senses that were reacting in an extraordinary manner to nothing more than a man's voice, Emily reminded herself. She spent her working life objective and detached…yet now, when it really mattered—when Miranda's recording contract was at stake—she was allowing herself to be sideswiped off-beam by a few simple words. 'I'm sorry, Mr…er—'

'Bussoni,' he supplied evenly.

'Mr Bussoni,' Emily said, her assurance growing behind the protection of the screen. 'I'm afraid I didn't give the gentleman who works for you a very warm welcome—'

'Really? He said nothing of it to me.'

She was beginning to get a very clear picture of the man now. The image of a hunter sprang to mind…someone who was waiting and listening, using all his senses to evaluate his quarry. 'I understand you'd like to discuss the possibility of signing the band?' she said carefully.

There was another long pause, during which Emily formed the impression that the man was scanning all her neatly arranged possessions, gathering evidence about her and soaking up information—drawing conclusions. And from his position in front of the mirror he could do all of that—and still keep a watch on her hiding place.

Taking over last minute from Miranda meant she had been forced to come straight from work. There had been no time to find out about the event, let alone who might be in the audience. She had certainly not anticipated the need to be on her guard—to hide everything away. 'You are from Prince Records?' she prompted in a businesslike tone, hoping to bounce the man into some sort of admission.

'Do you think you could possibly come out here and discuss this in person?'

It was a reasonable enough suggestion. But Miranda was never seen without full war paint, and after liberal applications of cold cream Emily's own face had returned to its customary naked state. If she hoped to impersonate her twin an appearance right now was out of the question.

'I know this must sound rude, after you've taken the trouble to come backstage, but I'm rather tired this evening. Do you think we could talk tomorrow?' she said, knowing Miranda should have recovered and taken her rightful place by then.

'Tomorrow afternoon, at three?'

Emily's hearing was acutely tuned to his every move. He was already turning to go, she realised. Suddenly she couldn't even remember what she had on the following day, let alone specifically at three o'clock in the afternoon. The only thing she was capable of registering—apart from an over-active heartbeat—was that the recording contract for Miranda's band was vital.

'OK. That's fine,' she heard herself agreeing. 'But not here.'

'Anywhere you say.'

Possibilities flooded Emily's mind. She dismissed each one in turn…until the very last. 'Could you come out to North London?' Her mother and father had insisted that if Miranda's cold had not improved by tomorrow she should be brought home to recuperate. Emily knew she could rely on her parents to fill in any awkward gaps…smooth over the cracks when she changed places with her twin.

'I don't see why not.'

'That's if you're still interested?'

Interested? Alessandro thought, curbing his smile just in case Miss Weston decided to suddenly burst out from her hiding place. If he had been fascinated before, now he was positively gripped.

He ran one supple, sun-bronzed finger down the slim leather-bound diary he so longed to open, and traced the length of the expensive fountain pen lying next to it before toying with a pair of cufflinks bearing some sort of crest.

The handbag on the seat had quality written all over it, rather than some flashy logo. And the smart black suit teamed with a crisp white double-cuffed shirt hanging on a gown rail was Armani, if he wasn't mistaken.

His gaze swept the threadbare carpet that might once have been red to where a pair of slinky high-heeled court shoes stood next to a dark blue felt sack, ornamented with a thick tassel. Alongside that, a pull-along airline case—

'Mr Bussoni?'

His gaze switched back to the screen.

'Mr Bussoni, are you still interested?'

There was just a hint of anxiety in the voice now, Alessandro noted with satisfaction. This contract obviously meant a great deal to her. He cast a look at the discarded stage costume... Something jarred. No, he realised. Everything jarred.

'Only on one condition,' he said, adopting a stern tone as he assumed the mantle of time-starved recording executive.

'And that is?' Emily said cagily.

'That you come to supper with me after our meeting.' Alessandro was surprised when a curl of excitement wrapped around his chest as he waited for her answer. 'You may have questions for me, and there's sure to be a lot we have to discuss,' he said truthfully, satisfied that he had kept every trace of irony out of his voice.

Emily let the silence hang for a while. Miranda would definitely have to be better by then, she thought crossing her fingers reflexively. 'That's fine,' she confirmed evenly. 'I'll let the rest of the band members know—'

'No,' the voice flashed back assertively. 'It only needs one person to take in what I have to say…and I have chosen you, Miss Weston. Now, are you still interested in progressing with this matter, or not?'

'Of course I'm interested,' Emily confirmed, suddenly eager to be free of a presence that was becoming more disconcerting by the minute.

'That's settled, then. I'll write my number down for you. Perhaps you'll be good enough to get in touch first thing… leave the address for our meeting with my secretary?'

'Of course.' She felt rather than heard him prepare to leave.

'Until tomorrow, Miss Weston.'

'Until tomorrow, Mr Bussoni.'

Emily held her breath and tried to soak up information as the door opened, then shut again silently. The man might have three humps and a tail, for all she could tell, but her body insisted on behaving as if some lusty Roman gladiator had just strolled out of the room after booking her for sex the next day.

After he'd left it took her a good few minutes to recover her equilibrium. And when she moved out from behind the screen everything seemed shabbier than she remembered it, and emptier somehow, as if some indefinable force had left the room, leaving it all the poorer for the loss.

By early afternoon the next day, Emily had cancelled all her appointments for the rest of the week and was ready to take her sister back to their parents' house.

Drawing up outside the front door on the short gravel drive, she switched off the engine and tried for the umpteenth time to coax her twin into facing reality.

'This man is different to anyone I've ever encountered before. It would be a real mistake to underestimate him, Miranda.'

'He made quite an impression on you, didn't he?' Miranda replied, slanting a glance at her twin.

'I didn't even see him properly,' Emily replied defensively. 'And don't change the subject. It's you we're talking about, not me.'

After assuming a low-profile role in an orchestra for a number of years, Miranda had attracted the attention of a leading Japanese violin teacher. In order to fund the lessons Emily's twin had started a band—a band that in the beginning had taken up only the occasional weekend; a band that was now taking up more and more of her time...

'I only need this recording contract for a year or so,' she said now, as if trying to convince herself that the scheme would work. 'Just long enough for me to launch my career as a solo violinist.'

Emily frowned. She wanted to help, but only when she was confident Miranda understood what she was letting herself in for. 'Are you sure Prince Records understands that? They would have grounds to sue if you let them down.'

'They won't have any trouble finding someone to replace me; the boys are great—'

'I'm still not happy,' Emily admitted frankly. 'I just can't see what you'll gain going down this route.'

'Money?' Miranda said hopefully.

Emily shook her head as she reasoned it through aloud. 'You're not going to be able to honour a recording contract drawn up by a man like Mr Bussoni and put in the practice hours necessary to study the violin with a top-flight teacher like Professor Iwamoto.'

'It won't be for long,' Miranda insisted stubbornly, unfolding her long limbs to have a noisy stretch. 'I'll cope.'

Before Emily had a chance to argue Miranda was out of the smart black coupé and heading up the path.

'Don't be silly,' Emily said, catching up with her sister at the front door. 'The more successful the band, the less likely it is that this crazy idea of yours will work. I know the money would be great, but—' The expression on her twin's face made Emily stop to give her a hug. 'I know you're still pining over that violin we saw in Heidelberg.'

'That was just a stupid dream—'

'Well, I don't know much about violins,' Emily admitted, 'but I do know what a sweet sound you produced on that lovely old instrument.'

'Something like that would cost a king's ransom anyway,' Miranda sighed despondently. 'And it's sure to have been sold by now.'

Emily made a vague sound to register sympathy while she was busy calculating how much money she could raise if she sold her central London apartment to the landlord who already owned most of the smart riverside block, and then rented it back from him. Miranda need never know. It was a desperate solution, but anything was preferable to seeing her sister's opportunity lost. 'If I can help you, I will,' she promised.

With a gust of frustration, Miranda hit the doorbell. 'You do enough for everyone already. You won't even let me pay rent—'

'If I didn't have you around, who else would keep the fridge stocked up with eye masks?' Emily demanded wryly.

Their banter was interrupted when the door swung open.

'Girls—'

Then another idea popped into Emily's head. 'I've got some investments—'

'No!' Miranda said, shaking her head vehemently. 'Absolutely not.'

'You're not arguing,' their mother said wearily, giving them both a reproving look.

'Heated discussion, Mum,' Emily said as she shut the door behind them. 'Where's Dad?'

'In his study, of course.'

Of course. Emily stole a moment to inhale deeply, taking in the aroma of a freshly baked cake coming from the kitchen, along with the gurgle of boiling water ready for tea.

'You look tired,' her mother said softly, touching her arm. 'And as for you, Miranda—' Her voice sharpened as if her maternal engines had revved to a new pitch. 'What you need is a good dose of my linctus, and a hot cup of tea—'

'Did I hear the magic words?'

'Dad!' the girls cried in unison.

After giving them both a bear hug, Mr Weston linked arms with his daughters and followed their mother into the kitchen.

'It will be easy for you, Emily,' her mother asserted confidently, after Miranda had outlined her plan to secure the recording contract. 'You're not emotionally involved like Miranda. And you'll run rings around this record company man when it comes to securing the best terms for Miranda.'

Emily was surprised by her reaction to this vote of confidence. It was unnerving to discover that her mother's assessment of the situation could be so far off the mark. Intuition told her that running rings around Alessandro Bussoni was out of the question. But her main worry was the strange way her heart behaved just at the thought of him joining them in the tiny house. The man behind the voice would fill every inch of it with presence alone, never mind the unsettling possibility that she might brush up against him—

'Are you sure you're all right with this, Emily…? Emily?'

Finally the concern in her father's voice penetrated Emily's dream-state, and her eyes cleared as she hurried to reassure him. 'Of course, Dad. Leave it to me,' she insisted brightly, 'I can handle Signor Bussoni—'

'Italian!' her mother exclaimed, showing double the interest as she unconsciously checked out her neat halo of curls. 'How exciting. And when did you say he was arriving?'

'Right now, by the looks of it,' Emily's father said as he peered through the window.

CHAPTER TWO

'OH, NO!' Miranda gasped, looking to her sister for guidance.

'Stay upstairs until he's gone,' Emily suggested briskly. 'I'll come and get you when the coast's clear. Mum. Dad. Act normal.'

'Yes, dear,' her mother said breathlessly, exchanging an excited glance with her father.

Don't look so worried,' Emily called after Miranda. 'I promise not to turn anything down without your approval.'

Exchanging quick smiles, the girls were just on the point of parting at the foot of the stairs when they stopped, looked at each other, and then swooped to the hall window.

Standing well back from the glass, Emily ran a finger cautiously down the edge of the net curtain.

'Oh, boy,' she murmured, watching the tall, darkly clad figure unfold his impressive frame from the heavily shaded interior of a sleek black car.

'You said Herman Munster,' Miranda breathed accusingly.

'I said he might have been Herman Munster for all I could see of him,' Emily corrected tensely.

'Looks like you were both wrong in this instance,' their father commented dryly.

* * *

Alessandro felt a frisson of anticipation as he double-checked the address his private secretary had passed on to him that morning.

He wasn't used to waiting, and eighteen hours was far too long in this case.

But then he wasn't used to speaking to someone hiding behind a screen either, or accepting anyone's terms but his own—which was how he now found himself getting out of a rented Mercedes outside a perfectly ordinary semi-detached house in North London.

He smiled a little in amused acceptance. He couldn't recall a single instance of being turned down by a woman, let alone agreeing to a time of her choosing for an audience as begrudging as this one. His sharp gaze took in the small rectangular lawn, freshly mowed, and then moved on to the splash of vivid colour provided by a pot of petunias to one side of the narrow front door. For someone who moved between palaces, embassies or the presidential suite in some luxury hotel when he was really slumming it, this chance to sample suburbia was a novelty… No. A welcome change, he decided as he swiped off his dark glasses.

Behind a snowy drift of net, the Weston family watched Alessandro Bussoni's progress towards the house in awe-struck silence.

'He's absolutely gorgeous,' Miranda murmured. Their distracted mother barely managed a weak gasp of, 'Oh, my!'

'Go, before he sees you,' Emily suggested urgently, having already turned her back on the window.

'But your make-up,' Miranda said, hopping from foot to foot, torn between going and staying.

Emily's hand shot automatically to her face. 'What about it?'

'You're not wearing any,' Miranda exclaimed with concern.

'Can't be helped. He'll still think I'm you. Why shouldn't he? Anyway, you're not wearing any make-up,' Emily pointed out.

'Only because I'm sick.'

'Well, there's no time for me to do anything about it now,' Emily said firmly. 'I'll be fine. Don't worry about me.'

'Sure?' Miranda asked hopefully.

'Sure,' Emily said briskly, hoping no one had noticed that her hand was shaking as it hovered over the doorknob.

'I'm going to change,' Miranda shouted, on her way up the stairs. 'Then I'm taking over from you.'

'No!' But even as Emily's gaze raked the empty landing to call her sister back she knew it was too late. Sucking in a deep, steadying breath, she seized the doorknob tightly and began to turn…

'You go and wait in the lounge, pet.'

'Dad—'

'Go and compose yourself,' Mr Weston urged gently, refusing to let go of her arm until Emily allowed him to steer her away from the door. 'You look like you could do with a few minutes. I'll keep him busy until you're ready.'

'You're an angel,' Emily whispered, reaching up on tiptoe to give her father an affectionate peck on the cheek. But a moment alone was all it took her to realise that she couldn't go ahead with the charade after all, and she rushed upstairs to find her sister.

The twins waited motionless, hardly daring to breathe as they stood just inside the door to Miranda's bedroom. It felt as if the conversation downstairs had been going on for ever while their father satisfied himself as to their visitor's identity and then invited him into the house, but at his signal they started down the stairs.

Emily was dressed in her customary relaxing-at-home-uniform of blue jeans and a simple grey marl tee shirt. Her well-buffed toenails, devoid of nail varnish, were shown off in a pair of flat brown leather sandals, while her long black hair was held up loosely on top of her head with a tortoise-shell clip.

In complete contrast, Miranda had somehow found enough time to coat the area around her large green eyes with copious amounts of silver glitter, add blusher to her cheeks and staggeringly high platform shoes to her seemingly endless legs.

Surely there could be no mistake, Emily thought, giving her twin the final once-over before they reached the sitting room door. Signor Bussoni would immediately presume it was Miranda he had seen on stage. 'Relax,' she whispered, taking hold of her twin's wrist. 'It'll be all right.'

'Then why are you shaking?' Miranda remarked perceptively.

'Girls? What's keeping you? You've got a visitor.'

'We're coming now, Dad,' Emily called back, hoping she sounded more confident than she felt. She had no idea what she was up against, and had nothing to go on but that disconcerting voice. For all she knew it might be Herman Munster hiding behind that impressive physique and those super-sleek clothes.

'Come on, love. What's the hold-up?' Popping his head round the door, her father drew her into the room. 'Your mother will have tea ready in about fifteen minutes,' he said. 'You two know each other,' he added, with an expectant smile.

Emily felt as if her powers of reason had vanished. Her mind's eye wasn't simply unreliable, it was positively defective, she decided, gazing up into a man's face that was almost agonising in its perfection. Thick ebony-black hair, cut slightly longer than was customary in England, was swept back and still tousled from the wind. Conscious he would think her rude, she forced her gaze away, only to discover lips that were almost indecently well formed and the most expressive dark gold gaze she had ever encountered.

Restating his name with a slight bow, Alessandro viewed the two sisters standing one behind the other. 'Miss Weston,' he murmured.

Lurching forward in response to Emily's none too subtle prompting, Miranda extended her hand politely. 'Delighted to see you, Signor Bussoni,' she said, letting out an audible sigh when Alessandro raised her hand to his lips.

'And I you,' he said in a voice as warm as the sunlight that had tinted his skin to bronze. 'But, forgive me, it is the other Miss Weston I have come to see.'

'The other Miss Weston?' Miranda squeaked, looking helplessly behind her to where Emily was standing rigid, wishing the ground would swallow her up.

'Indeed,' Alessandro said in a voice laced with humour. 'You did invite me, Miss Weston,' he said, looking straight at Emily.

Shock rendered both sisters speechless, and for a moment no one moved or spoke. If their own parents couldn't tell them apart, how could Signor Bussoni? Emily wondered tensely. She breathed a sigh of relief as her mother breezed into the room.

'Ah, Signor Bussoni, what a pleasure it is to have you in our midst.'

'The pleasure is all mine, I assure you,' Alessandro said, inclining his head towards the older woman in an elegant show of respect.

'I see you've met my girls.' Looking from Emily to Miranda, she clearly couldn't contain herself another moment. 'Have you heard Miranda play yet?' she said expectantly. 'The violin,' she prompted, when Alessandro stared at her blankly. 'Her interpretation of the Brahms "Violin Concerto" is second to none, you know. She won a competition with that piece.'

Emily's face flared hot as she realised that her mother was completely oblivious to the tension building around her.

'The violin?' Alessandro's face betrayed nothing but polite enquiry, but beneath the surface his mind was working overtime. Had he been hoist by his own petard? His plan had seemed audacious enough, but this family appeared intent on embroiling him in something even more ambitious. He glanced again at the girl her mother had called Miranda. Her provocative clothing and extravagantly made up face marked her out as a showgirl…but apparently she was a classical violinist. And then his gaze switched to the fresh-faced beauty he had come to see…the angel with the faintly flushed cheeks and the incredible jade-green eyes who masqueraded as a showgirl by night… To say the contrast intrigued him was putting it mildly. But what the hell was he getting himself into? Taking another look at Emily, he found he could not look away. He would have carried right on staring, too, had it not been for her sister's protestation providing him with a distraction.

'Oh, Mother, really,' Miranda said now, looking at Emily to back her up. 'Signor Bussoni doesn't want to hear about all that—Emily, say something.'

Emily, Alessandro mused, running the name over and over in his mind and loving its undulating form, its perfect proportions, its old English charm… Emily, Emily— Her mother fractured his musings with terrier-like determination.

'Emily won't stop me telling Signor Ferara all about your wonderful talent, Miranda. If no one speaks of it, how will you ever play that violin you so loved in Heidelberg?'

'Mother, please,' Emily cut in gently. 'I imagine Signor Bussoni's time is very precious. He's come here to talk about recording contracts for Miranda's band. I'm sure there will be other occasions when he can hear her play the violin.'

'Oh…' Mrs Weston hesitated, looking from one to the other in frustration.

'That would give me the greatest pleasure,' Alessandro agreed. 'But it was you I heard singing last night,' he stated confidently, turning to Emily, his bold gaze drenching her in the sort of heat she had only read about in novels.

'Emily took over for me because I caught a cold and lost my voice,' Miranda confessed self-consciously. 'As a rule, no one can tell us apart.'

'I see,' Alessandro said, nodding thoughtfully as he studied Emily's face. He would have known her anywhere…even if there had been five more identical sisters lined up for his perusal.

Emily tried hard to meet his stare, but he disturbed her equilibrium in a profound and unsettling way.

'Singing is just a hobby for me,' she started to explain. 'You would have signed up the band right away if Miranda had been onstage—'

'Possibly,' Alessandro murmured, confining himself to that single word while his eyes spoke volumes about his doubt. He couldn't have cared less if Emily had a voice like a corncrake…and beauty was in the millimetre, he realised, as he filled his eyes, his mind and his soul with the face and form of a woman he desired like no other. Emily Weston was everything he wanted…everything he needed to set his plan in motion. No, much more than that, he realised, and only managed to drag his gaze away from her when the telephone shrilled and everyone but he made a beeline for the door.

'Let me,' Emily's father insisted calmly, easing his way through the scrum.

'Won't you sit down, Signor Bussoni?' Mrs Weston said awkwardly. 'Miranda, go and fetch the tea tray.'

'Do you mind if I—?' Swaying a little, Miranda stopped mid-sentence and passed a hand over her forehead.

'You've still got a fever. You really should go to bed,' Emily observed, taking hold of her twin's arm. 'You'll never get better if you don't rest. I'll see her upstairs,' she said, turning to her mother. 'If you'll excuse me for a moment, Signor Ferara?' she added to Alessandro. 'I'll come down and serve the tea,' she promised, ushering her sister out of the door. 'Just as soon as I see Miranda settled.'

'That won't be necessary.'

Alessandro's voice stopped Emily dead in her tracks.

'You're not going—' she said quickly…far too quickly,

she realised immediately, noting the spark of interest in his eyes. Her heart thundered as he shot her an amused, quizzical look. 'Well, we haven't discussed the contract yet,' she said, attempting to make light of her eagerness for him to stay.

'Emily,' Miranda murmured weakly, 'I really think I should…'

'Of course,' Emily said, welcoming the distraction as she looped an arm around her sister's waist. 'Let's get you to bed.'

'Can I help?' Alessandro offered.

'That won't be necessary,' Emily said, urging her sister forward.

'Emily's right, Signor Bussoni,' Miranda murmured faintly. 'I'll feel better after a short rest. My sister has my full confidence. I am quite content for you to put your proposition to her.'

Alessandro answered with a brief dip of his head. 'I feel equally confident that your sister will find my proposal irresistible, Miss Weston.'

'I'm very grateful to you, Signor Bussoni,' Miranda replied as she stood for a moment, framed by the door, her carefully made-up face illuminated by an oblique shaft of late-afternoon sunlight.

Beautiful, Alessandro thought dispassionately, and if you stripped away the paint and glitter almost a carbon copy of her sister. But there was no attraction there. None at all. Not for him, at least.

'You will sort it out for me, won't you, Emily?' Miranda said anxiously as they left the room together.

'When have I ever let you down?' Emily teased gently as they started up the stairs.

'Never,' Miranda said softly, turning to give her sister a kiss.

Emily came back into the room to find Alessandro comfortably ensconced on the chintz-covered sofa, with her mother beside him chatting animatedly. But the moment she arrived his focus switched abruptly.

'Do you handle all your sister's business affairs?'

Emily prided herself on her ability to recognise exceptional adversaries on sight. And she was facing one right now, she warned herself. 'Not all,' she said carefully. She saw his eyes warm with amusement and knew he had her measure, too.

'Just contracts?' he pressed.

Emily's heart gave a wild little flutter, like a bird trapped in an enclosed space.

'We're not here to talk about me, Signor Bussoni—'

'Alessandro, please,' he said, embellishing the instruction with a small shrug intended to disarm, Emily guessed, as she watched her mother's eyes round in approval at what she clearly imagined was an enchanting display of Latin charm. But her mother had missed the shrewd calculation going on behind that stunning dark gold gaze, Emily thought, feeling her own body respond to the unmistakable masculine challenge.

'I'm sure you're very busy, Signor Bussoni,' she said, struggling to sound matter-of-fact with a heart that insisted on performing cartwheels in her chest. 'And it's the contract for Miranda's band you've come to discuss after all.'

'Correct,' he agreed.

His voice streamed over Emily's senses like melted fudge. How could a voice affect you like that? she wondered. Surely the cosy little room with its neatly papered walls had never housed such a dangerous sound as Alessandro Bussoni's deep, sexy drawl.

'It seems you and I have rather a lot to discuss, Miss Weston,' he said, reclaiming her attention. 'Far more, I must confess, than I had at first envisaged. I'll send my car for you at eight this evening.'

As he stood the room shrank around him.

'But surely you will stay for tea, Signor Bussoni—?'

'No—' Emily almost shouted at her mother. 'I'm sorry,' she said, instantly contrite. 'But Signor Bussoni must have other appointments—' was that a note of desperation creeping into her voice? She made a conscious effort to lower the pitch before adding, 'It's enough that he's making time to discuss Miranda's future tonight, Mother.'

He inclined his head to show his appreciation of her consideration.

'Until this evening, Miss Weston.'

'Signor Bussoni,' Emily returned with matching formality.

'Alessandro,' he prompted softly.

Emily felt her gaze drawn to dark, knowing eyes that seemed to reach behind her own and uncover the very core of her being. She felt deliciously ravished by them and immediately on guard, all in one and the same confusing moment.

A thrill ran through her as he lifted her hand and raised it to his lips. The contact was brief, but it was enough for her logical brain to be set adrift and her veins to run with sweet sensation. Then her father returned from his telephone call and she was able to take refuge behind the bustle of departure, easing into the background as Alessandro strode back down the path to his car.

Was he psychic? Emily wondered, as the unmistakable figure emerged from the grand entrance and came down the hotel steps at the precise moment the limousine she was arriving in swept to a halt outside.

Nothing would have surprised her about Alessandro Bussoni, Emily realised as he beat both the doorman and the chauffeur he had sent to collect her to the car door. As it swung open her mouth dried, and her body felt as if it was contracting in on itself in a last-ditch attempt to conceal anything remotely capricious in her appearance, though she had taken the precaution of wearing an understated navy blue suit with a demure knee-length skirt.

'Welcome, Miss Weston,' he said, reaching into the limousine to help her out.

Or to stop her escaping? Emily thought in a moment of sheer panic when his fingers closed over her hand.

'Please. Call me Emily,' she managed pleasantly enough, while her thought processes stalled.

Precaution, my foot! She should have worn a full protective body suit…with ski gloves, she reasoned maniacally, as a flash of heat shot up her arm. What was she thinking? The first rule of business was to keep everything cordial but formal. And here she was, unbending already as if she was on a date! Gathering herself quickly, she removed her hand from his clasp at the first opportunity.

'I must apologise for not coming to pick you up in person, Miss Weston,' Alessandro said, standing back to allow her to precede him through the swing doors.

Emily made some small dismissive sound in reply, and was glad of the distraction provided by a doorman in a top hat who insisted on ushering her into the hotel. But she was so busy trying to keep a respectable distance from her host she almost missed his next statement.

'I wanted to come myself, but there were some matters of State I was forced to attend to: matters that demanded my immediate attention—'

'Matters of State?' Emily repeated curiously. But it was hard to concentrate on what he was saying when they were attracting so much interest.

When the first flashbulb flared she glanced round, imagining some celebrity was in view. But then she realised that the cameras were pointing their way, and a small posse of photographers seemed to be following them across the lobby.

She smiled uncertainly as she tried to keep up with Alessandro's brisk strides. 'It must be a quiet night for them,' she suggested wryly.

'What? Oh, the photographers,' he said, seeming to notice

their presence for the first time. 'I'm sorry. You get so used to them you hardly know they're around.'

Having seen a pack of photographers waiting around on the night of the charity event, snapping away at anything and everything, even the spectacularly ornate heels on one woman's shoes, Emily took it for granted that hotels of this calibre attracted the attention of the world's media as a matter of course.

'I suppose they have to do something while they're waiting for the main event to arrive.'

'Main event?' Alessandro quizzed as he broke step to look at her.

'You know...personalities, showbiz people, that sort of thing.'

He pressed his lips together and he gave her an ironic smile, his dark eyes sparkling with amusement. 'I guess you're right. I'd never thought of that. It must get pretty boring for them...all the hanging around.'

But it wasn't just the photographers, Emily thought. She couldn't help noticing all the other people staring as Alessandro ushered her across the vast, brilliantly lit reception area.

Hardly surprising, she decided, shooting a covert glance at her companion. He was off the scale in the gorgeous male stakes. His dark suit was so uncomplicated, so beautifully cut, it could only have come from one of the very best tailors...yet somehow the precision tailoring only served to point up his rampant masculinity. His crisp, cotton shirt, in a shade of ice blue, was a perfect foil for his bronzed skin, and somehow managed to make eyes that were already incredible all the brighter, all the keener—

She looked away, knowing she would have to pull herself together if the evening was to fulfil its purpose as a business rather than a social occasion. 'Matters of State?' she repeated firmly, determined not to let him off the hook.

She was rewarded with a low, sexy laugh that revealed nothing except for the fact that she was fooling herself if she imagined that she would be able to overlook the power of his charm for one single moment.

At a small, private lift, tucked away out of sight from the main lobby, she watched as he keyed in a series of numbers. Heavy doors slid silently open and then sealed them inside a plush, mirrored interior. There was even a small upholstered seat in the corner should you require it, Emily noted with interest, and apart from the emergency intercom a telephone for those urgent calls between floors. The only users of this exclusive space would be pretty exclusive themselves, she deduced with a thoughtful stare at her companion.

'You didn't answer my question yet,' she prompted.

'I've taken the liberty of ordering a light supper to be delivered to us later.'

He might have said it pleasantly enough, but the effect was offset by a flinty stare that suggested that he alone would direct the course of their conversation.

Alessandro knew he was in for a rocky ride the moment he saw the defensive shields go up in Emily's eyes. And no wonder she thought him harsh. He was struggling to reclaim control of a situation that was slipping away from him as fast and as comprehensively as sand through a sieve. Logically, all he had to do was bring her to the point where she would sign the contract drawn up by his lawyers, but she had turned everything on its head, this woman he felt such a crazy compulsion to woo.

'Rather than go out to eat I thought it better that we devote ourselves entirely to the matter in hand,' he said, hoping to placate her. The last thing he wanted was to explain what this was about in a lift!

'You said something about matters of State earlier,' Emily pressed doggedly, 'and, if you remember, I asked—'

Words had always been the most effective weapon in her armoury, but where Alessandro Bussoni Ferara was concerned they seemed utterly ineffectual. Emily was starting to seethe with exasperation.

'So, what's this?'

In the split second between her lunge to grab his wrist and Alessandro's reaction to it Emily knew she had made her biggest mistake. What on earth was she doing, assaulting a strange man in a lift, snatching hold of him, grabbing on tight to the gold signet ring on his little finger? And why was he allowing her to hang on to him, even though he was twice her size and could have moved away from her in an instant? Worse still, the flesh beneath her sensitive fingertips felt warm and smooth and supple— She blinked, and recovered herself fast, removing her hand self-consciously from his fist where it had somehow become entangled.

'It's my family crest,' he volunteered evenly. 'Does that satisfy your curiosity?'

No! Not nearly! 'Your crest?' she said curiously.

His whip-fast retaliation left Emily with no time to hide the cufflinks on her own white tailored shirtsleeves.

'Shall we start with your explanation for these?' he countered smoothly, bringing her wrist up.

The sheer power in his grip was impossible to resist. But Emily found she didn't want to, and incredibly, was softening. 'That's my—'

'Yes?' he pressed remorselessly.

'My cufflinks are engraved with the crest of my Inn of Court,' she admitted, averting her face.

'Ah,' he murmured, as if pleased to hear his suspicions confirmed. 'Barrister?'

Emily nodded tensely. 'And you?'

Now it all made sense, Alessandro realised—the tasselled sack to hold her robes and wig, the pull-along airline case to transport her briefs, along with all the other papers she would have to carry around…the severe cut of the restrained outfit she wore to court beneath her gown hanging up in her dressing room at the hotel while she sang that night, the only nod to feminine sexuality displayed in the power heels of her plain black court shoes—

'This is our floor,' he said as the lift slowed.

Another evasion! Controlling herself with difficulty, Emily hunted for something…anything…to derail her mounting irritation—unfortunately, the first thing she hit upon was how well the light, floral perfume she had chosen to wear mingled with Alessandro's much warmer scent of sandalwood and spice, and that didn't help at all! As the lift doors opened she sprang to attention, noticing that he stood well back to let her pass. Now she registered disappointment. Disappointment that he didn't yank her straight back inside the intimate lift space, close the doors and make it stop somewhere between floors…for a very long time indeed.

'Emily? Did you hear me?'

Refocusing fast, she saw that he had already opened the arched mahogany double doors to his suite and was beckoning her inside.

'I'm sorry—'

'I said,' he repeated, 'would you care for a glass of champagne?'

'Oh, no, thank you. Orange juice will be fine until we conclude our business.'

'And then champagne?'

'I didn't say that, Signor Bussoni—'

'Alessandro.'

'Alessandro,' Emily conceded. 'And when our business is concluded I will be leaving.'

'Whatever you like,' he agreed evenly. 'I've no wish to tangle with lawyers in my free time.'

The throwaway line ran a second bolt of disappointment through her. She would have to be under anaesthetic not to register the fact that Alessandro Bussoni was a hugely desirable male. It was time to tighten the bolts on her chastity belt, Emily told herself firmly, if she had a hope in hell of being ready for what promised to be a tough round of business negotiations.

And she would deal with the lazy appraisal he was giving her now how, exactly?

She only realised how tense she had become when Alessandro turned away to pour them both a glass of freshly squeezed orange juice and each of her muscles unclenched in turn. Keep it cool, Emily warned herself silently. Cool and impersonal. It's only business after all…

CHAPTER THREE

LEAVING her handbag on the pale, grey-veined surface of a marble-topped console table, Emily dragged in a deep, steadying breath as she took in her surroundings.

The hotel room was decorated in English country house style, but at its most extreme, its most sumptuous: a symphony of silks, cashmere, damask and print. And Alessandro's accommodation wasn't just larger than the usual suite, it was positively palatial. In fact, Emily guessed the whole of her parents' house would fit comfortably into the elegant drawing room where they were now holding their conversation—a room that at a rough estimate she judged to be around forty feet in length.

'Not very cosy, is it?'

His voice startled her, even though it was pitched at little more than a murmur.

'Sorry?' she said, turning around.

'This room,' Alessandro said, holding her gaze as he carried the juice over to her.

'It's very—'

'Yes?' he said, noticing how studiously she avoided touching his hand as he passed her the crystal glass.

'Well…' Emily chose her words carefully. She didn't want to cause offence—maybe he loved this style. 'It tries very hard—'

'—to condense all the flavours of your country into a single room in order to impress the well-heeled tourist?' he supplied, looking at her with amusement over the top of his glass.

'Well, yes,' Emily said, discovering that a smile had edged on to her own lips. 'How did you guess? That's my opinion exactly.' Nerves were making her facial muscles capricious, unpredictable…and somehow she found herself smiling up at him again.

'Let's hold our meeting somewhere more…snug,' Alessandro suggested. 'Don't look so alarmed,' he said, shooting her a wolfish grin that failed entirely if it was meant to reassure her. Thrusting a thumb through the belt-loop of his black trousers, he slouched comfortably on one hip to put his glass down on the table. 'My bedroom can hardly be described as snug—it's almost as large as this room. Fortunately there are two bedrooms, and I've had the smaller of the two turned into an office for the duration of my stay.'

'I see,' Emily said, watching him extract some documents from the folder on the table and wondering why all she could register was how tanned, and very capable his hands were—

'Daydreaming again, Emily?'

'I beg your pardon?'

'And I beg you to pay attention when I ask you if you would care to join me in my office—so that our meeting can begin.'

His tone was amused—tolerant. And her expression must have been blank and dreamy, Emily realised, hurriedly adopting an alert look.

'Shall I lead the way?'

Retrieving her handbag, Emily hurried after him, but as he opened the door to the next room, and stopped beside it to let her pass, she juddered to a halt. The remaining space inside the doorframe was small…too small.

The difference in size between them seemed huge, suddenly, though it was his aura of confident masculinity that was his most alluring feature, Emily thought as she skirted past him. 'Very impressive,' she managed huskily, pretending interest in all the high-tech gizmos assembled for his use in the skilfully converted bedroom.

'Why don't you sit over there?' he suggested, pointing towards a leather button-backed seat to one side of a huge mahogany desk.

Perching primly on the edge, Emily watched in fascination as Alessandro sat or rather sprawled on his own chair with all the innate elegance of a lean and hungry tiger.

'Would you care to open the discussion?' he invited.

Folding her hands neatly in her lap, Emily attempted to sweep her mind clear of anything but the facts. 'Well, as you know, I'm here to secure the best possible deal for my sister's band—'

'For your sister, primarily?'

'Well, yes, of course, but—'

'Miranda needs the money a recording contract will bring her in order to buy a rather special violin and to complete her training, is that correct?'

'That's putting it rather crudely.'

'How else would you put it, Emily? What I want to know is, what's in it for me?'

'Surely that was self-evident when you saw the band perform. They're excellent—'

'Without you?' he cut in abruptly. 'How do I know what they'll be like? What if I said I'd sign the band if you remained as lead singer?'

'I'm afraid my obligations at work would not permit—'

'Ah, yes,' he cut in smoothly. 'I'll come to that later. But for now let's consider your proposal regarding the recording contract for your sister. How does she intend to fulfil both her commitment to the record company and to her tutor at the music conservatoire?'

'I'm here to ensure that whatever contract she signs allows her to do both—for the first year at least.'

'And then she will drop the band?' Alessandro suggested shrewdly.

'She will fulfil all her contractual obligations,' Emily stated firmly. 'I can assure you of that.'

'As well as put in the necessary practice hours to become a top-class international soloist? Somehow I doubt it,' he said, embroidering the comment with a slanting, sceptical look.

'You clearly have no experience of what it's like to strive to achieve something so far out of reach,' Emily said, over-ruling her cautious professional persona in defence of her sister, 'that most people would give up before they had even started.'

'Perhaps you're right—'

'Many artistes are forced to take other jobs to pay their way through college,' she continued passionately, barely registering Alessandro's silent nod of agreement.

'Not just musicians or artistes—'

But Emily was too far down the road either to notice his comment or to hold back. 'You're making assumptions that have no grounds in fact,' she flung at him accusingly.

'And you're not even listening to me,' Alessandro replied evenly, 'so how do you know what I think?'

'You've already decided she can't handle both commit-ments,' Emily said, realising she hadn't felt this unsteady since delivering her first seminar as a rookie law student. 'Right now, Miranda's not feeling well. But as soon as she's feeling better I know she'll do everything she says she will.'

'You say—'

'Yes, I say,' Emily said heatedly. 'I know my sister better than you…better than anyone—' She broke off, suddenly aware that all the professional expertise in the world was of no use to her while her emotions were engaged to this extent.

'I'm sure you're right,' Alessandro agreed quietly, showing no sign of following her down the same turbulent path. 'But why on earth choose a band as a way of making money? Why not find it some other way?'

Emily made an impatient gesture as she shook her head at him. 'Because she's a musician, Alessandro. That's what she does.'

'A cabaret singer?'

'What's wrong with that?'

As he shrugged, Emily guessed every stereotypical piece of nonsense that had ever been conceived around nightclub singers was swirling through his brain.

'Miranda makes an honest living,' she said defensively. 'Would you rather she gave it up…gave up all her ambitions…just to satisfy the prejudice of misguided individuals?'

Alessandro confined himself to a lengthy stare of good-humoured tolerance, and then held up his hands when a knock came at the door just as Emily was getting into her stride. 'Excuse me, Emily. I won't be a moment.'

As Alessandro left her Emily felt a warning prickle start behind her eyes. No one had ever made her lose her temper like this before…not once. She hadn't ever come close. Plunging her hand into her handbag, she dug around for some tissues, then rammed them away out of sight again when he came back.

'Come on, Emily,' he said, staying by the door. 'Supper's arrived.'

'I think I'd better go.' She resorted to hiding her face in a hastily contrived search for the door keys in her handbag.

'After supper,' Alessandro insisted as he held out his hand to her.

Was she meant to take it? Emily wondered as she stared up at him in surprise.

'Come,' he repeated patiently.

It was tempting. Maybe supper would give her a chance to relax, regroup, gather what remained of her scattered wits. She was here for Miranda, wasn't she? And the job she had come to do wasn't nearly finished. Eating was harmless…civilised. Lots of deals were cut over power breakfasts and business lunches; she'd done it herself on numerous occasions.

Romantic suppers?

Muffling the tiny voice of reason in her head, Emily convinced herself that the meal was nothing more than a brief interlude, a welcome break that would give her the chance to get her professional head screwed on ready for the discussions to come. But when she walked back into the first room she saw that a great deal more than a light snack awaited her.

'When you said supper, I imagined…' Her voice tailed off as she surveyed the incredible feast that had been laid out for them along the whole length of a highly polished mahogany table.

'Aren't you hungry?' Alessandro demanded, cruising along the table, grazing as he went. 'I know I am.'

She tried not to notice the way he seemed to be making love with his mouth to a chocolate-tipped strawberry.

'You can eat what you want when you want,' he said, sucking off the last scrap of chocolate with relish. 'And we can keep on talking while you do,' he added, his curving half-smile reaching right through her armour-plated reserve to stroke each erotic zone in turn. 'Would you like me to make a few suggestions?'

Withdrawing the plundered stalk from between his strong white teeth, he deposited it neatly on a side-plate.

Emily forced her mouth shut, but kept right on staring at him.

'Food?' Alessandro offered with an innocent shrug as he cocked his head to one side to look at her.

'That's fine, I can manage,' Emily said, almost snatching one of the white porcelain plates from his hands.

'Shrimp, *signorina*?'

'Don't you ever take no for an answer?'

The look he gave her sent a flame of awareness licking through every inch of her body.

'Relax, Emily. I deliver what I promise—just a light snack, in this instance.'

'I'm perfectly relaxed, thank you,' Emily retorted, concentrating on making her selection from the platters of delicious-looking salads…a selection she was making with unaccustomed clumsiness, thanks to the route her thoughts were taking.

Was it her fault that those beautifully sculpted lips provided a rather different example of a tasty snack…or that stubble-darkened jaw? Not to mention the expanse of hard chest she supposed must reside beneath his superior-quality jacket and shirt—and, talking of superior quality, what about the muscle-banded stomach concealed beneath that slim black leather belt? Distractedly, she spilled half a bowl of coleslaw on top of the mountain of food she seemed to have absent-mindedly collected on her plate.

'I don't think the pudding will fit,' Alessandro pointed out, removing a serving spoon holding a heaped portion of sherry trifle from her hand.

'Of c-course not,' Emily stammered, while the erotic mind games kept right on playing—ignoring her most strenuous efforts to put all thoughts of whipped cream and tanned torsos out of bounds.

When later she found herself drawn towards a tower of honey-coloured choux balls drizzled with chocolate, he asked, 'Do you like chocolate, Emily?'

'I love it. Why?' she said suspiciously.

Alessandro shrugged as he piled some profiteroles onto a plate, adding some extra chocolate sauce and pouring cream for her. 'We have a chocolate festival in Ferara every year; free chocolate is handed out all over the city. We even have a chocolate museum—you should make time to see it.' As he handed her the plate his amused golden gaze scanned her face. 'What do you say?'

'Thank you.' Was she accepting an invitation to consume a plate of delectable pudding, or something rather more?

'Imagine this, Emily—a thousand kilos of delicious chocolate sculpted into a work of art before your very eyes; artists coming from all over Europe to compete for a prize for the best design—'

He turned to pour them both a steaming cup of strong dark coffee from an elegant silver pot.

'Clean sheets are placed underneath each block so that the onlookers can help themselves to slivers as they watch—' He stopped, and stared straight into her eyes, his expressive mouth tugging up in a grin. 'Well?'

Emily's pulse-rate doubled. 'No cream, no sugar,' she blurted, certain he intended to provoke her—a chocolate festival, for goodness' sake!'

Murmuring her thanks as he pressed the coffee cup into her hand, she glanced up, only to encounter a dangerous gaze alive with laughter. She was right to be wary, she realised, looking away fast.

But thankfully this was his final sally, and he allowed her to finish her meal in peace. When they returned to his luxurious bedroom-turned-office, he kept the lights soothing and low as he slipped a CD into the music centre.

Emily smiled. Brahms, she realised, surprised he had remembered her mother mentioning Miranda's competition piece.

He poured champagne and brought two crystal flutes across before settling himself down on the opposite sofa.

'Better?' he murmured, watching her drink. 'Do you mind if I take my jacket off?' he added, loosening a couple more buttons at the neck of his shirt.

'Not at all,' Emily said, forgetting her pledge to keep champagne celebrations until later as she watched him ease up from the chair to slip off a jacket lined with crimson silk. Freeing a pair of heavy gold cufflinks from his shirt, he dropped them onto the table and rolled up his sleeves to reveal powerful forearms shaded with dark hair. There couldn't have been a more striking contrast to the type of pasty-faced executive she was accustomed to dealing with.

'So, Emily,' he challenged, eyes glinting as he caught her staring at him. 'Do you still think I'm one of those misguided individuals you referred to?'

For his opinion of cabaret singers, yes; where everything else was concerned—

'I take it from your expression that you do.'

His smile had vanished.

'Let's get one thing straight between us before we go any further. I don't give a damn what people do, as long as they're not hurting anyone else in the process. But I do care about motives—what makes people tick. What makes you tick, Emily?'

Racing to put her brain back in gear, the best she could manage was a few mangled sounds.

'Barrister by day,' he went on smoothly, 'moonlighting as a cabaret singer by night. There's no harm in that, if you can cope with the workload. And it's even more to your credit that you were moonlighting to help your sister out of a fix. What is not to your credit, however, is the fact that you intended to deceive me. Why was that, Emily?'

'I admit things got out of hand—'

The lame remark was rewarded by a cynical stare.

'You really thought you could pull this off?' he demanded incredulously. 'What kind of a fool did you take me for?'

Emily's face burned scarlet as she struggled with an apology. 'I didn't know you—I'm really sorry. I didn't think—'

Alessandro held up his hands, silencing her. 'As it happens, you're not the only one who hasn't been entirely straightforward.'

'Meaning?'

'Let's consider this plan of yours first.'

'My plan?' It was clear he was on a mission to tease out

her motives whilst taking care not to reveal any of his own, Emily realised.

'Amongst your misconceptions is the notion that your sister's crazy scheme is actually going to work.'

'Will you help her or not?'

'Without my co-operation your sister will never play the instrument she has set her heart upon.'

'What do you mean?' Emily said anxiously, finding it impossible to sit down a moment longer.

Stretching his arms out across the back of the sofa, Alessandro tipped his head to look at her. 'Why don't you sit down again, Emily?' he suggested calmly. 'You do want to help your sister, don't you? You do want her to be able to play that violin she saw in the instrument maker's shop near the castle in Heidelberg?'

Emily could feel the blood draining out of her face as she stared at him. 'How do you know about that?' she said in a whisper.

'I make it my business to know everything relevant to a case before I enter into any negotiation,' he said steadily. 'I never leave anything to chance.'

Emily's professional pride might have suffered a direct hit, but the only thing that mattered was Miranda's future… But what was Alessandro Bussoni really after? Why had he gone to so much trouble? And how did he come to have such a hold over a German violin maker?

'The violin in Heidelberg—' she began, but her voice faltered as she remembered Miranda playing the beautiful old instrument. 'What did you mean when you said that my sister might never get to play it?'

'Without my co-operation,' Alessandro reminded her, his expression masked in shade.

'I don't understand.'

'Sit down again, Emily. Please.'

'I think you owe me an explanation first.'

'The particular instrument you refer to is a museum piece almost beyond price. It was being displayed by one of today's most celebrated instrument makers—'

'*Was* being displayed?' Emily asked. 'Why are you talking about it in the past tense?'

'Because it's no longer there,' he said evenly.

'You mean it's gone back to the museum?' Relief and regret merged in the question.

'Not exactly.'

'What, then?' Her look demanded he answer her fully this time.

But Alessandro still said nothing, and just stared at some point over her left shoulder.

Slowly Emily turned around, her eyes widening when she saw what he was looking at. A beautifully upholstered taupe suede viewing seat was angled to face a large entertainment system. Nestled in the corner of the unusual triangular-shaped seat rested a violin, propped up between two cream silk cushions. 'Should it be out of its case?' she mumbled foolishly, sinking down on the sofa again.

'I imagine that's the only way it's ever going to be played,' Alessandro said, levelling a long, steady gaze at her.

Emily's heart was thundering so fast she could hardly breathe. She had to turn round to take another look, just to make sure she wasn't dreaming—to prove to herself that she really was in the same room as the violin Miranda had played in Heidelberg.

'But you told me it was a museum piece—beyond price,' she said, not caring that her battered emotions were now plainly on show. 'I don't understand.'

'Everything has its price Emily,' Alessandro said with a small shrug as he regarded her coolly.

He was waiting. For what? For her to say something? But how could she when her brain had stalled with shock and her whole body was quivering from some force beyond her control? To make matters worse, Emily couldn't rid herself of the idea that she too was a prize exhibit—and with a rather large price tag dangling over her nose.

'You bought it?' she managed finally.

'I bought it,' Alessandro confirmed.

'But why on earth—?'

'As a bargaining counter.'

'A bargaining counter?' Emily spluttered incredulously. 'What are you talking about?'

'Will you allow me to explain?'

Emily clenched and unclenched her hands. She didn't like the look on his face one bit. 'I think you better had,' she agreed stiffly, feeling as if she was clinging to Miranda's dream by just her fingertips now.

'It would be far better for your sister if she had enough money to continue her studies without the distraction of working with the band.'

'Well, of course,' Emily agreed. 'But—'

Alessandro's imperious gesture cut her off. 'Let me finish, please. It would be better still if she could have the use of that violin behind you—'

'Is this before or after she wins the Lottery?' Emily demanded, rattled by his composure.

'What if I told you that I am prepared to give the violin to your sister…on permanent loan?'

A thundering silence took hold of the space between them—until Alessandro's voice sliced through it like a blade. 'Well, Emily, what do you say?'

'What would she have to do for that?' Emily demanded suspiciously.

'Your sister? Nothing at all.' Alessandro's mouth firmed as he waited for Emily's thought processes to crest the shock he had just given her and get back up to speed.

Emily's eyes clouded with apprehension as her brain cells

jostled back into some semblance of order. 'What would *I* have to do?'

A smile slowly curled around Alessandro's lips, then died again. She was so bright…so vulnerable. It was as if he had spied some rare flower, moments too late to prevent his foot crushing the life out of it.

Standing up, he crossed the room. He needed time to think…but there was none. Opening a door, he reached inside the small cloakroom where he had been keeping the flowers. He had ordered the extravagant bouquet to seal their bargain. As he grabbed hold of them he realised that his hand was shaking. He paused a beat to consider what he should do. He could ram them in the wastebin, where they belonged, or he could keep on with the charade…

Turning to face Emily, he held out the huge exotic floral arrangement. There was real hope in his eyes, and a sudden tenderness to his hard mouth.

'I'm sorry, Emily, I meant to give these to you earlier.' She looked so wary, and Alessandro knew he was the cause. What had started out as a straightforward business transaction had developed into something so much more. If Emily Weston accepted his proposal he would be the luckiest man in Ferara… No—the world, he thought, trying to second-guess her reaction.

'For what?' Emily said, glad to have the opportunity to bury her face deep out of sight amongst the vivid blooms as he handed them to her. 'I've never seen such a fabulous display,' she admitted, forced to pull her face out again when they began to tickle her nose.

'For agreeing to become my wife,' Alessandro said softly.

For a full ten seconds neither of them seemed to breathe, and then Emily whispered tensely, 'Are you mad?'

Alessandro's rational self gave a wry smile, and told him she might be right. But thirty generations of accumulated pride in Ferara insisted that no woman in her right mind would refuse the opportunity to become princess of that land.

'Not as far as I am aware,' he said coolly.

'I think you must be.'

'I said I had a proposition for you. I made no secret of it.'

'Yes, a recording contract…for my sister—from Prince Records,' Emily said, thrusting the bouquet away from her as if she felt that by accepting it she was in some way endorsing Alessandro's plunge into the realms of fantasy.

'I have no connection whatever with any company called Prince Records,' he said, brushing some imagined lint from the lapel of his jacket.

'What?'

'You assumed I was a recording executive,' he elaborated. 'I allowed you to go on believing that…while it suited me.'

'I see,' Emily said, finding it difficult to breathe. 'And now?'

'The deception is no longer necessary,' Alessandro admitted. 'Because I have something you want and you have something I want. It's time to cut a deal.'

Emily felt as if her veins had been infused with ice. She might be twenty-eight and unmarried, but when her prince came along she wanted more than a business deal to seal their union…she wanted love, passion, tenderness and a lifetime's commitment—not a charter of convenience to close a cold and cynical deal. 'So, who the hell are you?' she demanded furiously.

'Crown Prince Alessandro Bussoni di Ferara,' he said. 'I know it's rather a mouthful—Emily?'

Snapping her mouth shut again, Emily whacked the bouquet into his arms. 'Take your damn flowers back! My sister might be in a vulnerable position right now, but let me assure you, Alessandro, I'm not.'

'Your sister put herself in this position—'

'How dare you judge her?' Emily flared, springing to her feet to glare up at him. 'You don't have the remotest idea how hard she works!'

Alessandro felt as if he had been struck by a thunderbolt,

and it had nothing to do with the fact that no one—absolutely no one—had ever addressed him in this furious manner in all his life before.

Just seeing Emily now, her eyes blazing and her hair flung back, her face alive with passion, intelligence and a truckload of determination, he felt a desperate urge to direct that passion into something that would give them both a lot more pleasure than arguing about her sister.

Was he falling in love? Could it be possible? Or was he already in love? Alessandro forced a lid on the well of joy that threatened to erupt and call him a liar for wearing such a set and stony expression in response to her outburst, when all he wanted to do was to drag her into his arms and kiss the breath out of her body. Had the thunderbolt struck the first moment he saw her, commanding that gaudily decorated stage…putting the harsh spotlights to shame with her luminous beauty—a beauty that had refused to stay hidden even under what had seemed to him at the time to be half a bucket of greasepaint?

'If you'll excuse me, I'll go and call my car for you,' he said steadily, revealing nothing of his thoughts. 'I can see you're upset right now. We will discuss this tomorrow, when you are feeling calmer—'

'Don't waste your time!' Emily snapped defensively.

'With your permission,' Alessandro said, swooping to retrieve the discarded bouquet from the floor by her feet, 'I'll have these couriered to your mother.'

'Do what the hell you want with them!'

But as she calmed down in the limousine taking her safely home through the damply glittering streets, Emily was forced to accept that without financial assistance Miranda would never achieve her full potential. A grant might be found to cover her lessons with the Japanese violin professor, but no one was going to stump up the funds necessary to buy her a violin of real quality.

But how could marriage to a stranger provide the answer? She gave her head an angry shake, then began to frown as she turned Alessandro's preposterous suggestion over in her mind. With the right controls in place it might be possible…it would certainly secure Miranda's future.

The ball was in Alessandro's court. If he was serious he wouldn't be put off by her first refusal; he would be back in touch with a firm proposition very soon… *Very soon.* How long was that? Emily wondered, feeling a thrill of anticipation race through her.

CHAPTER FOUR

EMILY'S family sat in a closely knit group on the sofa in front of her, their faces frozen with disbelief.

'And so we'll all board Alessandro's private jet and fly out to Ferara for the wedding,' Emily finished calmly.

Her mother recovered first. Glancing at the vivid floral display that took up most of the front window, she turned back again to Emily, her face tense with suppressed excitement. 'Are you quite sure about this?'

'Quite sure, Mother.'

'No,' Miranda said decisively. 'I can't let you do this for me.'

But as Miranda cradled the precious violin in her arms it appeared to Emily as if the wonderful old instrument had finally come home.

'Believe me, you can,' she said firmly, turning next to her father. 'Dad? Don't you have anything you'd like to say?'

Her father made a sound of exasperation as he wiped a blunt-fingered hand across his forehead. 'I've never understood this romance business. I just knew your mother was right for me and asked her to marry me. She accepted and that was it.'

'You can't mean you approve of this, Dad?' Miranda burst out, distracted from her minute inspection of the violin. 'Just because it worked for you and Mum doesn't mean it's

right for Emily. She doesn't even know this Alessandro
Bussoni—'

'Well, I only got to know your father in the first year,' their
mother pointed out. 'And Alessandro's a prince.'

As Miranda groaned and rolled her eyes heavenwards, her
father made his excuses.

'I have work to finish if we're all going off on this jaunt
next week.'

'A jaunt?' Miranda exclaimed, watching him hurry out of
the room. 'Doesn't Dad know how serious this is?'

'Alessandro has given me a cast-iron contract,' Emily said
calmly. 'I've read it through carefully and even had it double-
checked in Chambers.'

'And you're sure that Miranda's fees will be paid in full?'

Miranda flashed a look of dismay at her mother.
'Mother, really!'

Emily put a restraining hand on her sister's arm. 'Fees, as
well as a grant, Mother, plus an indefinite loan of the violin.'

'And the only way Alessandro's elderly father can abdicate
is if Alessandro marries you?'

'That's right, Mother. You see, we need each other.'

In spite of her bold assurances, Emily wondered if she
really was quite sane. She could recall every nuance of
Alessandro's telephone call—the call that had come through
almost the moment she'd walked into her apartment after
their meeting. He had signed off the deal with a generosity
beyond anything she could have anticipated. At least, those
were the tactics he had employed to make her change her
mind, she amended silently. Tactics. She rolled the cold little
word around her mind, wishing there could have been more—
wishing she could have detected even the slightest tinge of
warmth or enthusiasm in Alessandro's voice when he'd upped
his offer to ensure her agreement. But it had been just a list
of commitments he was prepared to make in exchange for her
hand in marriage. He might have been reading from a list—

perhaps he had been, Emily thought, trying to concentrate on what her sister was saying.

'And all you have to do is marry some stranger,' Miranda exclaimed contemptuously.

'Don't be like that,' Emily said softly.

Miranda made a sound of disgust. 'Well, I think you've all gone completely mad.'

Emily might have agreed, even smiled to hear the word she had so recently flung at Alessandro echoed by her sister, but noticing how Miranda held the violin a little closer while she spoke only firmed her resolve. 'This marriage lasts just long enough to allow Alessandro's father to abdicate in his favour and Miranda to complete her studies with Professor Iwamoto. That's it. Then it's over. So don't any of you start building castles in the air—'

'Castles,' her mother breathed, clapping her hands together as she gazed blissfully forward into the future. 'Who'd have thought it?'

'I'll make it work. I have to,' Emily said, when she was alone in her bedroom with Miranda later that day. 'I've got nothing to lose—'

'You've got everything to lose!' Miranda argued passionately. 'You might fall in love with Alessandro, and then what?'

'I'm twenty-eight and have managed to avoid any serious romantic entanglements so far.'

'Only because you're a workaholic and no one remotely like Alessandro has ever crossed your path before,' Miranda exclaimed impatiently. 'What are you going to do if you fall in love with him? He's one gorgeous-looking man—'

'Which makes it all the easier to keep the relationship on a professional level,' Emily cut in, seizing on the potential for disappointment. 'He's bound to be spoiled, selfish, inconsiderate and self-obsessed. Just the type of man I have always found so easy to resist.'

'And what if you get pregnant?' Miranda persisted.

'Absolutely no chance of that.'

'Now you do have to be kidding. You'll never be able to resist him. And Alessandro looks like one fertile guy—'

'It's never going to happen without sex.'

'What?' Miranda stared blankly at her.

'I've had it written into the contract,' Emily said, congratulating herself on her foresight. 'It seemed like a sensible precaution. And it saves any embarrassment for either party.'

'"It saves any embarrassment for either party",' Miranda mimicked, trying not to laugh. 'Get real! You'll never know what you're missing.'

'Exactly,' Emily confirmed. 'And I intend to go back to work when all this is over, so I don't need any distractions.'

'Alessandro isn't a distraction; he's a lifetime's obsession,' Miranda pointed out dreamily.

'Maybe,' Emily conceded. 'But he'll want out of this contract as much as I will do. Don't go making Mother's mistake and reading more into it than there is. This is a straightforward business deal that suits both of us. It's a merger, not a marriage.'

'Then I'm sorry for you,' Miranda said softly. 'For Alessandro, too. And it makes me feel so guilty—'

'Don't,' Emily said fiercely, clutching her sister's arm. 'Don't use that word. You have to support me, Miranda. It's too late to back out now. I've already arranged to take a career break. Just think—I'll be able to pay off my mortgage with Alessandro's divorce settlement, so you're helping me to achieve my dream, too.'

'In that case, I guess we're in this together,' Miranda said, pulling a resigned face.

'Just like always,' Emily admitted, forcing a bright note into her voice as she tried not to care that her marriage to Alessandro was doomed before it even began.

'Like for ever,' Miranda agreed, on the same note as her

twin. But her face was full of concern as she looked beyond Emily's determined front and saw the truth hovering behind her sister's eyes.

It was a beautiful summer's evening of the type rarely seen in England. The milky blue sky was deepening steadily to indigo, and it was still warm enough to sit out on the hotel balcony in comfort. The uniqueness of the weather was perfectly in accord with the mood of the occasion, Emily mused as she watched Alessandro come back to her with two slender crystal flutes of champagne. The business of signing the contract was over, and now it was time to celebrate a most unusual deal.

A little shiver ran through her as she took the glass. Marriage to a man like Alessandro would have been an intoxicating prospect whatever his condition in life... If there had only been the smallest flicker of romance—but there was none.

'To us,' he murmured, breaking into her thoughts with the most inappropriate toast she could imagine.

'To our mutual satisfaction,' Emily amended, only to find herself qualifying that pledge when she saw the look on his face. 'With the outcome of our agreement,' she clarified.

'Ah, yes, our agreement,' Alessandro repeated with a faint smile. 'It may not have been spelled out to you exactly, but you will be entitled to keep the title of Principessa if you so wish... Emily?'

'That's really not important—'

'Not important?'

She could see she had offended him. 'Look, I'm sorry. I—'

His dismissive gesture cut her off. Turning his back, he stared out across the rapidly darkening cityscape. 'Once we are married the title is yours for life, whether or not you choose to use it.'

'I will have done nothing to earn that right,' Emily protested edgily.

'Don't be so sure,' Alessandro countered, spearing her with a glance. 'There are bound to be difficulties before you settle into the role.'

'Please don't worry about me, Alessandro. I'm quite capable of looking after myself.'

Emily was convinced that she was right, but she hadn't reckoned with the speed with which Alessandro would put the plan into operation. By the end of the week even travel arrangements had been finalised. Emily and her family would fly to Ferara in Alessandro's private jet while he remained in London to conclude his business dealings there.

As the day of departure drew closer, the speed of change in Emily's life began gathering pace at a rate she couldn't control. It felt as if the carefully crafted existence she had built for herself was being steadily unpicked, stitch by intricate stitch. The first warning sign was when a young couple arrived unannounced to take her measurements and speak in reverent terms of Brussels lace and Shantung silk, Swiss embroidery and pearls. At that point Emily realised that if she didn't put her foot down she would have little to say even about the style of her own wedding dress. As if to confirm her suspicions, just a couple of days later clothes began arriving at her apartment—without anything being ordered as far as she was aware—as well as boxes of shoes by the trunkload.

Feeling presumptuous, almost as if she was attempting to contact someone she hardly knew, she picked up the telephone to call Alessandro at his London office.

She was so surprised when his secretary put her straight through that for a few moments she could hardly think straight.

'I know it's a bit crude,' he admitted, covering for her

sudden shyness with his easy manner. 'But time has been condensed for us, Emily, and I wanted you to feel comfortable—'

'Comfortable?' Emily heard herself exclaim. 'With clothes labelled "Breakfast, lunch, dinner: al fresco; breakfast, lunch, dinner: formal"! And that's only two of the categories. There must be at least a dozen more—'

'You don't like them?' Alessandro said, sounding genuinely concerned.

'I'm sorry. I don't mean to sound ungrateful.'

'Should we meet and discuss it, do you think?'

'Yes.' She should have pretended to think about his offer for a moment or two, she realised.

'Shall I come for you now?' There was a note of amusement in his voice.

'That would be nice,' she managed huskily.

Alessandro took her to lunch at one of the city's most exclusive restaurants. Somewhere so discreet that even a prince and his beautiful young companion could pass a comfortable hour or two consuming delicious food in a private booth well away from prying eyes.

Laying down her napkin after the most light *millefeuille* of plump strawberries, bursting with juice, sweetened with icing sugar and whipped cream, Emily wondered how she was going to refuse Alessandro's fabulous gifts without offending him.

'Is something troubling you?' he pressed, signalling to the waiter that he was ready to sign the bill. 'You surely can't still be worrying about those clothes?'

'I don't know what to think about them,' Emily admitted frankly, hiding her confusion behind the guise of practicality. 'There are just so many outfits—it would take me the best part of a year just to try them all on.'

'So leave it for now,' he suggested casually. 'Grab a few things you like, and I'll have the rest delivered to the palace.

You can take your time over them in Ferara. I just thought as we were in London it was too good an opportunity to miss.'

'You're very kind…too kind,' Emily said impulsively. Her heart was hammering painfully in her chest, while Alessandro's gaze warmed her face, demanding that she look at him.

'I just want you to be happy,' he murmured.

A muscle flexed in his jaw, as if he was struggling with the situation almost as much as she was. 'For the duration of the contract,' Emily said, as if trying to set things straight in both their minds.

Inclining his head towards her, Alessandro gave a brief nod of agreement. 'Talking of which—' Reaching inside the breast pocket of his lightweight jacket, he brought something out, then seemed to think better of it and put it back again.

'Are you ready to go?' he said, standing up. 'I thought we might take a stroll around the park before I take you back.'

As they left the restaurant Emily was aware that the same men who had followed them discreetly from her apartment were just a few footsteps behind them now.

'Don't worry,' Alessandro said, linking her arm through his, seeing her turn. 'They're the good guys.'

'Your bodyguards?'

'Yours, too, now that you are to be my wife,' he reminded her.

The thought that she was to be Alessandro's wife excited her, in spite of everything, but the thought that she would never go anywhere again without bodyguards was the flipside of the coin. She needed Alessandro to guide her through this confusing new world, Emily realised. There were so many things she had to ask him…

'Would you like to come back to my place for coffee?'

The few seconds before he replied felt like hours. So long, in fact, that Emily began to feel foolish—as if she had made some clumsy approach to a man she'd only just met.

'Better not,' he replied with a quick smile.

'Don't worry—I just thought—'

Alessandro could have kicked himself. Emily's invitation had been irresistible—almost. But if they went back to her apartment there could only be one outcome and, to his continued surprise, Emily Weston had awoken a whole gamut of masculine instincts within him—prime amongst which, at this moment, was his desire to protect her. To protect her, to woo her, and then make her his wife. And he had already accepted that the timing of that last part of his plan might not coincide exactly with their wedding day.

'There's still time for that walk in the park.'

They were sheltering from rain beneath a bandstand when he said, 'You'd better have this.'

'What is it?' Emily said curiously, watching as again he dipped his hand inside the breast pocket of his jacket. She frowned when she saw the ring he was holding out to her.

'It would cause quite a stir in Ferara if you weren't seen wearing this particular piece of jewellery,' Alessandro explained, as coolly as if it was a laptop that came with the job.

Of course there would be a ring…she should have known. And it was a very beautiful ring. But shouldn't an engagement ring be given with love…and with tenderness?

'Don't you like it?'

It really mattered to him, Emily realised, taking in the fact that the ring was obviously very old and must have been worn by Alessandro's ancestors for generations—possibly even by his late mother.

'If you prefer you could just wear it on public occasions.'

'I love it,' she said firmly. And I can see how much it means to you, her eyes told him. 'It's just with all these fabulous clothes, and now this…' The words dried up as he took hold of her hand. His expression was lighter, as if a great burden had been removed from his shoulders.

'Thank you,' he said softly. 'I was hoping you'd like it. It has been passed down through my family.'

'Tell me more,' Emily encouraged, forgetting everything else as she surrendered to Alessandro's voice, and his touch…but most of all to the sudden realisation that she wasn't the only one who needed reassurance.

'I know it isn't the usual huge and very valuable stone,' he began, 'and perhaps it isn't the type of thing you might have been expecting. But this ring has a provenance that no other piece of jewellery can boast.'

It might have been made for her, Emily realised as he settled it on her finger. Dainty ropes of rubies and pearls wound around the circumference with a ruby heart as the centrepiece of the design. 'Tell me about it,' she repeated.

'There was a Prince of Ferara named Rodrigo,' Alessandro began. 'He fell in love with a beautiful young girl called Caterina. Rodrigo had this ring made for her…'

As his voice stroked her senses Emily tried to remain detached and remind herself that Alessandro was only telling her a story. But it wasn't easy when her mind was awash with alternative images.

'On his way to ask for Caterina's hand in marriage, Rodrigo's horse shied, throwing him unconscious into the lake. Robbed of her one true love, Caterina decided to join a religious order.'

Emily tensed as Alessandro switched his attention abruptly to her face. 'What happened to her?' she asked quickly, full of the irrational fear that he could read her mind and know it was full of him rather than the characters he was telling her about.

'Caterina's horse shied on the way to the convent,' he said casually, the expression in his eyes concealed beneath a fringe of black lashes. 'When she recovered consciousness this ring was right there by her side.'

The ruby heart seemed to flare a response, making Emily gasp involuntarily.

'So, did she join the religious order?'

'She couldn't.'

'Couldn't?'

'That's right.'

'Why not?'

'I should take you home now, if you are to have an early night before your flight to Ferara tomorrow,' he said restlessly, as if he wished he had never started the story. 'I have another business meeting in about—' He frowned as he glanced at his wristwatch. 'About ten minutes ago.'

All the romance…all the tenderness…had vanished from his voice as if it had never been. Of course it had never been, Emily thought, angry for allowing herself to get carried away. Alessandro's fairy story was just part of the play-acting they were both forced to endure…and the ring was just another prop.

'I'll take good care of it,' she said, closing her fist around the jewel-encrusted band.

'I'm sure you will,' he murmured as he straightened up. 'Shall we go?'

It was an instruction, not a question, Emily realised. 'You don't have to see me home,' she said quickly. 'I've made you late enough already.'

'I'm taking you back,' he insisted in the same quiet determined tone that made it impossible to argue with him.

Alessandro left her at the door to her apartment, refusing yet another invitation to cross the threshold. *'Li vedro in Ferara, Emily,'* he said, waiting until she had closed the door.

'Yes. See you in Ferara, Alessandro,' Emily confirmed softly, turning away from him to face the empty room.

CHAPTER FIVE

IT SEEMED to Emily that everyone in Ferara had cause to celebrate apart from the main characters in the drama that was about to unfold.

From one of the windows in the turret of the huge suite she had been given for her few remaining days as a single woman she had a good view of the cobbled thoroughfare outside the palace walls. Bunting and banners in the distinctive Feraran colours of crimson, blue and gold hung in colourful swathes across the street, along with numerous posters of the soon to be married couple…Emily Weston and Prince Alessandro Bussoni Ferara. Es and As, intertwined.

For once Emily was forced to agree with her mother. It hardly seemed possible!

She had been awake since dawn, when all the unfamiliar sounds of a new day in Ferara had intruded upon her slumbers. Only then had she begun to drink in the unaccustomed luxury of her new surroundings—and with something closer to dread than exhilaration. The setting was everything she might have dreamed about—if she'd been a dreamer. One thing she had not anticipated was how it might feel to be set adrift in a palace that, however fabulous, was full of endless echoing corridors where everyone but she seemed to know exactly what was expected of them.

Ferara, at least, was far lovelier than she had ever dared to expect. On the drive from the airport the countryside that had unrolled before her had been picture-postcard perfect. A landscape of lilac hills shrouded in mist, some crowned with quaint medieval villages shielding fields cloaked in vines, and clusters of cypress trees standing on sentry duty against a flawless azure sky.

The Palace of Ferara was constructed around a sixth century Byzantine tower, and seemed from a distance to be balanced perilously on the very edge of a towering chalky-white cliff face. Rising out of the low cloud cover as they had approached by road, both palace and cliff had appeared to be suspended magically in the air. But as they'd drawn closer Emily had seen that the stone palace was both vast and set firm on towering foundations.

No wonder a Princess of Ferara needed so many clothes, she mused as she retraced in her mind those parts of the palace she had already been shown. The sheer number of rooms was overwhelming.

Tossing back the crisp, lavender-scented sheets, she swung her legs over the side of the bed and headed towards the glass-paned doors leading onto her balcony. Even in the early-morning sunshine the mellow stone already felt warm beneath her naked feet. Staring out across the city, she felt like an excited child, monitoring the progress of some promised treat… Except that she wasn't a child any longer, Emily reminded herself, pulling back. She would have to be totally insensitive not to realise that the people of Ferara had high hopes for this marriage, and all she had to offer them was a sham.

She dragged her thoughts from harsh reality and they turned inevitably to Alessandro, and how long his business would keep him from Ferara. The best she could expect was that he would turn up for their wedding. Then they would get on with their own lives—separately. She would stay on in Ferara, of course, and act out her part as promised. But what did Alessandro have planned? Would she see him at all?

Shaking her head, as if to rid herself of pointless speculation, she reached for the telephone and dialled an internal line.
After several rings she remembered that Miranda and her
parents would probably have already left for their promised
tour of Ferara.

So, what did a 'soon to be' princess do in her spare time?
Ring the office, she told herself, trying another number.

'Force of habit,' she explained to the uncharacteristically
bewildered Clerk of Chambers who normally organised her
working life with unfailing efficiency. 'Yes, OK, Billy. See
you at the wedding then.'

She tried to hang on to the familiar voice in her mind, but
when she replaced the receiver the room seemed to have
grown larger and even emptier than before she placed the call.

Shower, dress, and draw up a plan, she decided, trying to
ignore the stab of tears behind her eyes as she headed purposefully towards the lavish marble bathroom. She would have to
pull herself together and find a meaningful role for herself if
the next couple of years weren't going to be the longest of her
life.

She felt better when she came out of the bathroom, hair
partly dried and hanging wild about her shoulders, and with
a fluffy white towel secured loosely round her hips. She had
waltzed herself halfway across the ballroom-sized bedroom,
humming her own version of Strauss, before she realised she
was not alone. As her hands flew to tug up the towel and cover
her breasts she realised there wasn't enough material to cover
everything—

'Calm down. I'll turn my back,' Alessandro murmured
reassuringly.

It wasn't easy to stay calm when your heart was spinning
in your chest!

'Who let you in?' she said, backing up towards the door
of her dressing room.

'I apologise for arriving unannounced.'

He could try a little harder to *sound* contrite, Emily thought, conscious that her nipples had turned into bullets. 'I thought you had business to conclude in London.'

So did I, Alessandro mused wryly. But thanks to you, Emily, I couldn't stay away. 'Can I help you with that?' he offered, moving towards her as she debated whether to simply brazen it out and turn to open the dressing room door, or try to manoeuvre the handle with her elbow whilst clinging on to the towel and preserving what little remained of her dignity.

'That won't be necessary,' she said, choosing the latter option.

'Oh, come now, Emily,' Alessandro murmured, moving closer. 'I have seen a woman's body before…'

That was all the encouragement she needed to try and bludgeon the handle into submission with an increasingly tender arm.

'It's not as if anything's going to happen,' he added sardonically, 'remember that "no sex" clause?'

'Yes, thank you, I do remember,' Emily said, conscious that every tiny hair on her body was standing to attention.

'See? I'm not even looking,' he insisted, leaning across her to open the door. 'Your modesty is utterly preserved, *signorina*.'

Launching herself into the dressing room, Emily slammed the door shut and leaned heavily against it as she struggled to catch her breath.

'Don't be long,' Alessandro warned from the other side. 'I've got something to show you…something I think you might like.'

Emily's gaze tacked frantically around the room as she tried to decide what to do next. Dropping the towel, she sprinted naked to examine her daunting collection of new clothes.

Everything was cloaked in protective covers and there were photographs of each outfit on labels attached to the hangers; labels that came complete with directions as to where matching accessories might be found. But her investigations were hampered by too much choice. And just what was the appropriate outfit for after you'd stepped out of the shower only to be discovered naked by possibly the most delicious male on the planet? A male, furthermore, with whom you could anticipate no hanky-panky whatsoever!

Modest enough to prove you weren't the least bit interested in him, she decided, and casual enough to put them both at their ease.

Decision made, Emily dived into the bottom of the wardrobe and tugged out her trusty jeans and tee shirt.

'I hope you slept well?'

'Very well, thank you,' she replied politely, giving Alessandro a wide berth on her way back across the room. 'I had no idea you had arrived home.' Reaching the massive fireplace, she intended to rest one trembling arm on the mantelpiece, but missed when she found she couldn't reach. Acting nonchalant, she leaned against the wall instead, and levelled a bogus confident stare on Alessandro's face.

'Come over here,' he said softly, indicating the cushion next to his own on the cream damask sofa.

As one corner of his mouth tugged up in a smile Emily's battered confidence took a further plunge into the depths, while her heart seemed capable of yet more crazy antics. 'Why?' she said suspiciously.

'Because there's something that I'd like you to see,' he said patiently.

Emily took care to measure each step, so as not to appear too keen.

'Sit down,' he invited, standing briefly until she was comfortably settled on the sofa.

Maintaining space between them, Emily folded her hands out of harm's way in her lap and waited.

Reaching down to the floor at his feet, Alessandro brought up an ancient brown leather casket and set it down on the table in front of her. Releasing the brass catches, he lifted the lid. 'For you,' he said, tipping it up so that she could easily see the contents.

Emily gasped, all play-acting forgotten as she peered into the midnight-blue interior, where a quantity of diamonds flashed fire as the early-morning sunlight danced across their facets.

Reaching into the casket, Alessandro brought out a diamond tiara, together with earrings and a matching bracelet and necklace. 'You will wear these with your wedding dress,' he said, laying them out on the table in front of her.

'Don't you think that's a bit much?'

'To my knowledge, no Princess of Ferara has complained before,' he said, sweeping up one ebony brow in an elegant show of surprise.

'Well, I had planned a more restrained look—'

'You'll do as you're told,' Alessandro cut in firmly. 'The people of Ferara expect—'

'The people of Ferara,' Emily countered, 'are receiving short shrift from us both. And I can't…I won't appear any more of a hypocrite than I already am. They deserve better—'

'You will honour this contract,' Alessandro returned sharply, 'and leave the people of Ferara to me. They are my concern—'

'Shortly to be mine,' Emily argued stubbornly. 'If only for the duration of our agreement. While this contract runs its course,' she continued, 'I intend to fulfil my duties to this county, and its people, in full. And I warn you, Alessandro, I will not be side-tracked from my intended course of action by you.'

'Then you will do as I ask and wear this jewellery,' he insisted, clearly exasperated. 'It's for one day only. That is all I ask.'

Emily mashed her lips together as she thought about it.

The royal tiara to hold her veil in place and cement Alessandro's position as ruler of Ferara? She would agree to that. 'I would love to wear the tiara, but this ring is what your people care about,' she said, touching the ruby and pearl band. 'All the other jewellery is very impressive, but, just as you said, no jewel, however valuable, can boast the history of this one modest piece. Why overshadow it? I think your people would appreciate seeing simplicity in their Princess. I've no wish to flaunt your wealth.'

There was a long pause during which Emily couldn't fathom what was going on in Alessandro's mind. His face remained impassive, but behind his eyes myriad changes in the molten gold irises marked the course of his thoughts. Even sitting with his back to the sun, with his face half in shadow, the light in his eyes was remarkable, Emily mused, leaving tension behind as she slipped deeper into reverie.

'You're an exceptional woman, Signorina Weston—'

She started guiltily out of her daydream as Alessandro began putting the fabulous jewels back inside their velvet nest. She could hardly believe what he was saying…doing. She had won her first battle—and so easily— 'You agree?' she said, holding her breath.

'I agree,' Alessandro said, almost as if he surprised himself. 'Everything will be locked up for safekeeping. The tiara will be returned to you on the day of our wedding.'

'Thank you,' she said with relief, getting to her feet as Alessandro stood up to go. 'Will I see you again before then?' It was a question she longed to know the answer to…a question she knew she had no right to ask him.

'I imagined you would be too busy with your preparations,' Alessandro said, looking at her intently. 'I have meetings arranged right up to the morning of the ceremony…I thought I'd give you time to sort through all those clothes,' he added, clearly of the opinion that any woman should be thrilled by such a prospect.

But Emily wasn't impressed. As far as she was concerned, the over-abundance of outfits in her walk-in wardrobe represented nothing more than a selection of costumes for the short-running drama production in which she was about to appear.

'I'd like to do something worthwhile…learn something about Ferara,' she insisted. 'The clothes can wait.'

For a moment Alessandro seemed taken aback. 'Well, good,' he said. 'I'll find someone to have a chat with you—'

As her stomach clenched with disappointment, Emily's lips tightened. 'Don't bother,' she said tensely. 'I'll find someone myself.'

After eating breakfast alone in her suite, Emily knew it was time to make good her boast to find someone who would tell her a little about Ferara. Catching sight of an elderly gardener through one of her many windows, she hurried out of the room.

He was as gnarled as an oak tree and, right now, as bent as one of its branches as he leaned over the plants he was caring for. Emily remained discreetly half hidden as she stared at him, wondering if she had made the right choice.

She needn't have worried about disturbing him. He was oblivious to everything around him apart from the roses he was tending.

Emily smiled as she watched him. The old man's love for his plants was revealed in his every move. He had probably worked in the palace gardens most of his long life. Ferara was that sort of place. Who better to tell her everything she wanted to know? He might not speak too much English, but her Italian was…not too bad, she consoled herself. They should be able to have a conversation of sorts—and anything was preferable to returning to the silence that dominated her ornate, but ultimately sterile rooms.

'Buon giorno!' she began hopefully, walking towards the solitary figure. 'I hope I'm not disturbing you.'

'Not at all, *signorina*. I'm delighted to have the company.'

'You speak English,' she said, unable to keep the excitement from her voice.

'I do,' the elderly man replied, leaning heavily on the handle of his fork. 'What can I do for you, *signorina*?'

'Don't you feel the sun?' Emily said, shading her eyes with her hand. 'It's terribly hot out here.'

'Yes, I feel the sun,' he agreed. 'I love to feel the sun. I love to be outside…with my roses,' he elaborated, gesturing around him with one nobly hand whilst star-bright amber eyes continued to reflect on Emily's face. 'Do you like flowers?'

'I love them,' she replied.

'Roses?'

'Especially roses,' Emily sighed, as she traced a petal wistfully. 'They remind me of my parents' garden in England.'

'Do you feel homesick already?' he asked perceptively.

It was as if some bond formed between them in that moment. And as they smiled at each other Emily felt herself relax. 'I'm surprised they flourish here in this heat so late in the summer,' she said, reining back the emotion that suddenly threatened to spoil these first moments with a potential new friend and possible ally.

'My own system of filtered sunlight and judicious watering,' the old man told her proudly. 'Like me, these roses love the sun. And, like me, in this hot climate their exposure to it must be rationed. Otherwise we'd both shrivel up.'

He chuckled, and his eyes sparkled with laughter, but Emily could see the concern behind them, and regretted that she was the cause.

'What's this one called?' she asked, determined to set everything back on an even keel as she pointed to an orange-red, rosette-shaped bloom.

'A good choice,' he commented thoughtfully, stabbing his fork into the ground to come and join her. 'This rose is named after Shakespeare's contemporary, the great English playwright Christopher Marlowe. Here,' he invited, selecting a bloom to show her and holding it up loosely between his fingers, 'inhale deeply, *signorina*. You should be able to detect a scent of tea and lemon. Lemon tea,' he declared, chuckling again, pleased with his joke.

'Mmm. It is a distinctive scent,' Emily agreed after a moment. 'But what is the connection between Christopher Marlowe and roses?'

'You don't know?' he demanded.

It seemed as if she was going to have to learn something about her own culture before starting on his, Emily realised. 'I'm afraid I don't,' she said ruefully.

'Christopher Marlowe pressed a rose inside the pages of a book he gave to a friend after an argument…to express his regret over their disagreement.'

'And did his friend forgive him?'

'Who could resist?' the old gentleman retorted, his eyes widening as he surveyed the array of beautiful blooms nodding in the breeze in front of them.

Before Emily could stop him, he cut one for her.

'Here, *signorina*, take this. Press it between the pages of a book…and always remember that if a rose is shown love and care it will flourish and bloom, wherever it is planted.'

Taking the flower from his hand, Emily smiled. 'Do you work here every day?'

'I intend to,' he told her, eyes shining with anticipation. 'I intend to make this rose garden the most talked about in all of Ferara…all of Europe!'

They talked for some while, and then she left him to his work.

'I'm sure you will,' Emily agreed. 'It's so very beautiful already.'

'Would it bother you if I came here to talk to you again?'

'Bother me?' he exclaimed with surprise. 'On the contrary *signorina*. I should love it.'

'In that case,' Emily said happily, 'see you tomorrow.'

The old man bowed as she started to move away. 'Until tomorrow, *signorina*. I shall look forward to it.'

After her encounter with the elderly gardener Emily felt more confident that she had something to contribute to palace life. A plan was taking shape in her mind: a scheme to improve the living conditions of all Alessandro's employees—though she had to admit to a moment's concern when her private secretary said she knew of no one matching the old man's description in royal service.

Turning it over in her mind, Emily returned to her desk to catch up on some correspondence. On the top there was a large red journal she didn't recognise, and, opening it at the flyleaf, she saw it was from Alessandro. He had written simply, 'For Emily from Alessandro—a record of your thoughts'. And then, at the bottom of the page, he had added the date of their forthcoming marriage.

'Do you like it?'

She nearly jumped out of her skin. 'I love it,' she said bluntly, running the fingers of one hand appreciatively down the length of its spine.

'Your secretary showed me in,' he explained. 'I hope you don't mind?'

'Not at all.' The now familiar surge in her pulse-rate had reached new and unprecedented levels, Emily discovered as she continued to stare at Alessandro standing on the balcony outside her room. Surely there would come a point where she'd got used to seeing him? But how could anyone look that good in a pair of jeans and a simple dark linen shirt? She surmised he was off-duty, and wondered what he planned to do with his free time. 'Is this a gift for me?' she said, glancing down at the journal.

He answered with a grin and a shrug.

'Five years of entries?' she teased lightly. 'I presume you couldn't get any less?'

His silence allowed her to draw her own conclusions. 'Well, I've never had anything like it before.' she admitted frankly, 'so, thank you.'

'May I come in?' he said, leaning on the doorframe.

'Of course.' She wondered if her heart would ever steady again. 'I was only going to write some letters.'

'But I thought you wanted to have a look around Ferara?'

'I do.' She tried not to read anything into the remark, but her pulse rate rebelled again. 'I'm very keen to learn more. Actually, I've already made a friend of one of the gardeners.'

'Did he tell you much about our country?'

'He was a very interesting old gentleman, as it happens. And, Alessandro?'

'Yes?'

Emily waited, noticing how his eyes reflected his thoughts—there was a something in his expression now that suggested this might be a good time to air her idea. 'I know you've been very busy, and that small things aren't always apparent, but…'

'Get on with it,' he encouraged with a gesture.

'After talking to the gardener I got the impression that his apartment could do with some renovation—just some little touches that would make his life easier.'

'And you'd like to take charge of these?'

'Yes. I think it would be worthwhile.'

'I'm sure it would,' Alessandro agreed. 'And as far as learning more about Ferara is concerned—well, I've taken the afternoon off, so I could show you around, if you like.'

A shiver of excitement raced down Emily's spine as she let him wait for her answer.

'The chocolate festival,' he prompted, 'the one I told you about? It's usually held in February, but there's to be a special demonstration in celebration of our marriage. Because of the heat at this time of year it's taking place inside the grand hall of one of the municipal buildings.'

So, his talk of a chocolate festival hadn't been a wind-up after all, she realised, feeling a rush of anticipation. 'I'd love to go.'

'That's settled, then,' he said. 'We'd better leave right away if we want to catch the best demonstrations.'

When they arrived, Emily was amazed to find the streets of Ferara had been recreated within the cool, vaulted interior of the ancient building, complete with chocolate stalls, chocolate sculptures in various stages of completion, and crowds milling about. There was a ripple of excitement when Alessandro was spotted with his bride-to-be, but after the initial surprise they were able to move around the vast marble-floored exhibition area quite freely. It was Emily's first real exposure to her new countrymen, and at first she held back a little self-consciously, but Alessandro grabbed her hand, drawing her forward, giving every indication of being proud of his choice of bride.

He was either a very good actor, Emily decided, or—a very good actor, she told herself firmly, knowing how easy it would be to let her imagination get the better of her where Alessandro was involved.

'Let me get you some chocolate,' he offered, weaving through the press of people, towing her behind him. He took her to stand beneath one of the towering pillars where an artist was already busy at work, then reached out and caught some of the glossy flakes as they showered down. He began feeding them to her, until Emily had to beg him to stop.

'Stop? Are you sure?'

'No,' Emily admitted, laughing because she was sure her face had to be smeared with chocolate.

To anyone unaware of their tangled relationship they would have passed for two people in love, laughing and enjoying the festival for what it was—an explosion of happiness and goodwill to celebrate the marriage of a man who was clearly much loved by his fellow Ferarans.

Freed from the tensions imposed by their arranged marriage, they actually enjoyed each other's company, Emily realised, smiling ruefully as she accepted the clean handkerchief Alessandro produced from his pocket.

'Is there anything else you should have warned me about?' she probed cheekily. 'Cream bun fights, perhaps?' She gazed up at him as she tried to wipe some of the chocolate smears off her face, loving the feeling of closeness that had sprung up between them.

'I think I can safely promise you one or two more interesting customs throughout your time here.'

Emily's smile faltered. Trying not to spoil the mood, she shook herself out of the doldrums. 'Tell me about these different traditions,' she pressed with another smile.

'If you haven't guessed already, our wedding's a great excuse for giving some of the best a second airing. Everyone in Ferara loves a carnival. You'll definitely be seeing my country at its best.'

'I'm looking forward to it,' she said. And she was, especially if Alessandro was to be her guide.

'You're still covered in chocolate,' he commented as she made another attempt to clean her face.

'Well, if I am it's all your fault,' Emily countered with a laugh that swiftly turned into an uncertain silence.

That remark was the closest she had ever come to flirting with him. And in view of his comment that seemed to remind her of the time limit on her visit, flirting was out. Not only that, but her teasing manner was attracting quite a bit of interest. 'I must look a mess,' she said self-consciously.

'You look lovely,' Alessandro argued, removing the handkerchief from her hand. Dampening one clean corner with his tongue, he very gently wiped her face for her. 'There's—that's better,' he declared at last with satisfaction.

Emily fought the urge to stare into his eyes, suddenly terrified that what she might see there would not match her own feelings. 'I suppose we'd better be getting back.' She broke free and went to stand some distance away before he had the chance to put distance between them.

This was crazy, Emily realised. When all she wanted was to be with him here she was calling an end to the day almost before it had begun! How had she ever imagined she could throw herself in the path of a man like Alessandro and walk away unscathed? Suddenly she couldn't wait to get away. The smell of the chocolate, the heat of the crowd and the noise reverberating round the lofty building stabbed at her mind, and she was almost running as she burst out through the imposing double doors that led to the open air. Shielding her eyes against the unforgiving rays of the midday sun, for a moment she was completely disorientated. Starting down the broad sweep of stone steps, she nearly stumbled.

'Emily! Are you all right?'

The voice was unmistakable—deep, and concerned. Tears sprang to her eyes as he caught hold of her, and she hated herself for the weakness. Somehow she had to get back her pre-Alessandro control, Emily raged inwardly. But she needed his steadying arm to guide her down the steps...

'It's hot, and you've consumed vast quantities of chocolate,' Alessandro said soothingly. 'I think we should take a gentle stroll back to the palace. I'll organise a light lunch—'

'Oh, no. I couldn't eat anything,' Emily said truthfully, though her lack of appetite was a direct result of the ache in her heart; nothing at all to do with the sunshine or an over-abundance of chocolate.

'I think for once you're going to do as I say,' Alessandro said sternly as he led her carefully down the steps. 'You almost fell up there. Then what would I have done? I can't have a wedding without a bride.'

'I'm sure you'd find someone without too much trouble.'

'But they wouldn't be you, would they?' he said tolerantly.

'Does that matter?'

'Yes, it does. So you're just going to have to humour me. The sun is strong and you're not used to it. Here, lean on my arm. We'll take it slowly…walk in the shade. I don't suppose you've eaten properly.'

'I've had lots of chocolate,' she pointed out mutinously.

'An unrelieved diet of chocolate might get a little boring, even for you. A light salad, some iced water—'

She hoped he was right. Maybe the heat *was* getting to her…the heat, and feelings she was sure he didn't reciprocate. Alessandro was simply making the best out of a difficult situation, she thought, flashing a look up at him…while she was falling in love, she realised with a stab of concern.

Alessandro returned Emily's troubled glance with a smile and a reassuring squeeze. He had been right to take her out of the heat. He should have anticipated how many people would attend the event, but he had just wanted an excuse to be with her. The chocolate festival had been the perfect opportunity.

Falling in love had been the last thing on his agenda, he realised as they made their way slowly back to the palace. But here, under the centuries-old shade of the cypress trees, the warmth of the sun was like a balm that enveloped them both in its healing rays. If he could have done, he would have willed all the mistrust, all the uncertainty that had tainted their relationship to float away on the light breeze that sighed through the branches over their heads…

Emily was perfect, and the mood of his people was wholly supportive, he realised with pleasure as he courteously returned several greetings. She would make a wonderful first lady: a true equal to stand beside him and care for these people he loved so much. She could hardly wait to make a start on improving the lot of those around her…sharing her own happiness with others. He snatched a look at the woman who in one short week would be his bride. She was deep in thought, but not so preoccupied that she couldn't take account of every smile that came her way and return it with sincerity. He felt a rush of deep affection for her…something that transcended physical attraction and looped a band of love around his soul.

He had never once felt like this, Alessandro realised, relishing the simple trust she placed in him, linking her arm through his. The privilege of being allowed to care for her made him happier than he could ever have imagined. It fulfilled him…completed him. Falling in love with Emily was the most natural, the most inevitable step he had ever taken. But if he rushed things he knew he ran the risk of damaging their relationship, perhaps irrevocably. He would have to take things easy…take it slowly, give them both time to get to know each other.

It wasn't enough that the chemistry between them was almost frightening in its intensity and that every male instinct he possessed insisted he take her straight to his bed. He knew with utter certainty that if he wanted more, he had to wait—

'D'you know, Alessandro?'

She captured his attention so easily, he realised happily. 'Tell me,' he prompted softly.

'I love Ferara…I love your people… They're all so friendly, so genuine and so welcoming…' She hesitated.

'And?' he said gently, sensing there was something more she wanted to say.

'I really think this might work…between us,' she elaborated awkwardly, though there was no need, Alessandro thought with an inward smile as he drew her a little closer. He had already come to that same conclusion himself, some time ago.

CHAPTER SIX

FOR the next couple of days Emily hardly saw Alessandro, except in passing. But she knew he was swept up in protocol, and fine-tuning their wedding arrangements. Her own family was busy with last-minute preparations, too, so any spare time she had she spent talking to her new friend.

With only one night to go before the wedding, she finally found the courage to ask him more about where he lived. Now that she intended the welfare of the palace staff to be one of her main areas of interest while she was in Ferara, this looked like as good a time as any to make a start. 'Does it suit you?'

'Suit me?' he asked with a wry grimace.

'I'm sorry,' Emily said, realising he probably didn't have much choice. 'I suppose your accommodation comes with the job.'

His nod of agreement suggested she had hit the mark. Emily decided to press on. 'Are you comfortable there?'

'Not bad,' he agreed, after much thought. 'Though the kitchens are a long way from my apartment. By the time I get my food it's usually cold.'

'Don't you have your own kitchen?'

'My own kitchen?'

'A kitchenette?' she amended quickly. This new turn in her career was proving to be harder than she had expected. 'Somewhere to prepare yourself a bite to eat…a drink?'

'No. Nothing like that,' he told her, rubbing the back of his neck with his hand as he thought about it. 'Sounds like a good idea, though.'

'I'm sure I could arrange something for you.'

'Could you?'

'Would you let me try?'

'Only if you agree to give me cookery lessons as well,' he said, dismissing the idea with a wry grin and a flick of his hand.

'I'm not thinking of anything very elaborate,' Emily said encouragingly, 'just a small fridge, and perhaps a kettle and toaster to start with. If you had those, at least you'd be able to make yourself a quick snack whenever you felt peckish.'

'Good idea!' her new friend said enthusiastically. 'I'll leave it with you, then.'

'Excellent,' Emily said enthusiastically. 'I'll let you know what progress I've made when I see you tomorrow—'

'Tomorrow?'

Emily's hand flew to her mouth. 'My wedding day—' Her stomach churned with apprehension. How could time have passed so fast?

'So, where is your husband-to-be?'

'Prince Alessandro?'

'Yes, yes,' her elderly friend retorted impatiently. 'My son. Where is he? Why has he left you on your own?'

'Your—' Emily's mouth fell open as the full extent of her blunder overwhelmed her. 'You didn't say!'

'And would you have been so open with me if I had?' Alessandro's father demanded as he levelled a shrewd look on her face.

'Well…I…I don't know,' Emily admitted frankly. 'You must think me a terrible fool—'

'On the contrary,' he replied. 'I think you anything but a fool. My son, however—'

'Oh, no, please,' Emily said, shaking her head. 'You don't understand—'

'What don't I understand?' the old Prince demanded, straightening up so that even in his gardening clothes Emily could be under no misapprehension as to his status.

'I... Well... This is not the usual sort of wedding.'

'You love him?' he asked her directly.

'Well, I...' Emily paused, unsure of what to say.

'I said,' he repeated sternly, 'do you love my son?'

'Causing trouble again, Father?'

The deep, familiar voice went straight to Emily's heart. 'Alessandro!' she exclaimed breathlessly. Who said a prince could descend on you unannounced, wearing snug blue jeans and a close-fitting white top, looking as if he had just climbed out of bed? And his hair was still damp from the shower, she noticed on closer inspection.

'I see you've met my father,' he said, shooting her a wry grin.

He betrayed nothing of their developing friendship, but, remembering his concern for her after the chocolate festival, Emily felt a shiver of awareness shimmer over every part of her as he moved past her within touching distance. He had been more than tolerant. He had been... As she struggled to find the right word she watched him throw his arms around the older man and kiss him warmly on both cheeks several times before hugging him again. To be the object of such fathomless affection—to be capable of bestowing it—

She looked at Alessandro as if seeing him for the first time, and knew without question that she loved him.

'Papa! Mi sei mancato!'

His father's voice was equally fierce as he clutched his son to him. *'Anche tu, Alessandro.* I've missed you, too, *vagabondo!'*

Another hug and they were done, leaving Emily still gaping.

'You have neglected your bride so badly she has forgotten that tomorrow is her wedding day,' the old man accused, wiping his eyes on his sleeve. 'You are a bad boy, Alessandro—neglecting us both like this.'

'I never neglect you, Papa,' Alessandro argued, flashing a glance at Emily as he tightened his arm around his father's shoulder. 'It's just that business sometimes—'

His father pressed his lips together in a show of disapproval. 'Business, business, business,' he proclaimed with a dismissive gesture. 'And your bride, Alessandro? What about your bride?'

Emily was forced to laugh as Alessandro executed a deep bow, flashing her a smile as he straightened up. 'I can only offer you my most humble apologies, Signorina Weston. Whatever punishment you decide to exact, I shall accept without question.'

Don't tempt me, Emily thought, feeling the effects of his statement reverberate around her senses.

'Once again,' Alessandro continued easily, tossing her an amused and comprehending look, 'I regret that unavoidable matters arose, demanding my immediate attention—'

'Your *bride* demands your immediate attention,' his father broke in sternly. 'Your wedding is tomorrow, in case you had also forgotten that, Alessandro.'

'I had not forgotten, Father,' Alessandro responded softly, glancing at Emily.

'It doesn't matter,' Emily insisted, shaking her head to hide her confusion. 'Alessandro is very busy, Your Royal Highness. And I have plenty to occupy me,' she managed vaguely. 'I'll leave you two together—'

'You will do no such thing,' the old Prince informed her imperiously. 'You will stay here with me and talk a while longer. After tomorrow Alessandro may begin the process of taking precedence over me. But today, as far as I am aware, I am still the undisputed ruler of Ferara, and I wish to talk with my future daughter-in-law. Alone,' he added pointedly. 'Make yourself busy somewhere else, Alessandro. Emily and I have much to discuss.'

'Father,' Alessandro said, executing a small formal bow. 'Your wish is my command.'

The wedding had more similarities to a big-budget film than any ceremony Emily had ever attended before. And, in true cinematic fashion, preparations for her starring role began just before dawn, when her private secretary called to inform her that the beauticians and hairdressers had started to arrive.

Breakfast was delivered on a tray with legs, presumably so that she could enjoy her last breakfast as a single woman safely tucked up in bed. But Emily was already out and about when the young maid knocked timidly on the door. Together they decanted the fruit juice and croissants onto a table over-looking the rose garden.

'You can take the rest away. I shan't eat it,' Emily insisted ruefully, scanning the cooked delicacies and plates of cold meats and cheeses, knowing she couldn't face them. 'Oh. Leave me an orange,' she said as an afterthought. She knew they had come from the palace orchard and were absolutely delicious.

'Yes, *signorina*,' the maid said with a courteous bob.

Just as Emily had thought, her simple breakfast proved to be the only oasis of calm in a day that was testing in the extreme. Pulled from pillar to post, she found herself constantly surrounded by strangers all charged with seeking perfection. The unfamiliar attention was daunting, and what made it worse was being treated suddenly as if she was on a higher stratum from everyone else. It made normal conversation impossible.

As her hair was dressed up, ready to hold the weight of the tiara, and the finest film of coral rouge was applied to her cheeks, Emily began to feel increasingly like an inanimate object. No one seemed able to meet her eyes. No one spoke unless she instigated the conversation. And no one seemed prepared to volunteer an opinion on anything, preferring to wait for her to state her own views as if they were the only ones worth listening to. The lack of verbal interplay was driving her crazy. And her nerves were building to crisis level as what had been a theoretical exercise became all too real.

Just when she thought she couldn't stand one more minute of it, her face broke into a smile.

'Dad! Mum! Miranda!' Breaking free of the posse of primpers, Emily fled across the room towards her family.

'But, *signorina*…your veil,' the designer called after her.

'Give me a moment, please,' Emily said, keeping her head firmly buried against her father's shoulder.

'Five minutes,' her father bartered, keeping her close as he encircled Miranda's shoulders with his other arm. 'Then you can have her back, I promise.'

There was such quiet determination in his voice that even the highly-strung designer was forced to concede defeat.

Her father sounded just like Alessandro, Emily thought fondly, raising her head to watch the couturier make an imperious signal and lead his group out of the room.

'There's still time to change your mind, Emily,' Miranda whispered, looking around anxiously at their mother, who nodded agreement.

'It's not too late,' her father agreed gruffly. 'I can have you out of here in a jiffy—'

'No, Dad,' Emily insisted firmly. 'There's too much at stake here—for everyone concerned. I'm going ahead with it.'

'Oh, the violin arrived! It is absolutely—' Miranda's hand flew to her mouth. 'How could I mention that?' she asked herself distractedly. 'When you're having to put up with all this?' She made a wild gesture to encompass the various stations dotted around the room set up by hairdressers, beauticians and designers.

'It's not so bad,' Emily teased. 'No, honestly,' she said sincerely, catching hold of Miranda's hand. 'Nothing would induce me to stay here if I didn't want to. It's not so bad living here at the palace with Alessandro.' She raised her eyebrows a fraction as she looked at her sister.

'You mean—' Miranda flashed a glance at their mother and father, who quickly pretended interest in the view outside the window.

'No, I don't mean what you're thinking,' Emily said softly. 'But he's great fun to be with when you get to know him. And he's so kind.'

'Is that all?' Miranda said, sounding disappointed.

'It was never meant to be anything more,' Emily pointed out, working at her smile. 'And you look beautiful,' she said, desperately trying to turn the direction of the conversation. 'And Dad, Mum, you look fantastic,' she added for good measure.

'You're absolutely sure about this?' her father said, looking at her again with concern.

'Yes,' Emily said, raising her eyes to his to prove that her composure really was restored. 'You can call everyone back in again now. I'm ready.'

The ancient cathedral in Ferara was on so vast a scale it might have been built for some lost race of giants. As Emily arrived beneath the towering stone archway that marked the entrance a murmur rose from the congregation like a collective sigh.

'This situation is about as real as a film,' her father murmured, echoing Emily's thoughts. 'The only difference is, I doubt any of us will be able to forget this once the show's over.'

'Courage, Dad,' Emily replied as she squeezed his arm. 'We'll get through this together.'

'I'm supposed to be supporting you, remember?' he growled out of the side of his mouth as the opening chord burst from the organ and an angelic choir soared into the first anthem.

Emily was about to move forward when one of the several attendants who had joined the procession from the palace attracted her attention.

'*Signorina, scusami l'interrruzione,*' he murmured, bowing low. 'This is an ancient custom in our country. The bride's flowers are traditionally a wedding gift from the groom's family.'

'How lovely,' Emily said, exchanging her bouquet with a smile.

'His Serene Highness is most keen that traditions should be upheld,' the attendant added, backing away from her in a deep bow.

As Emily's curled her fingers around the slender stems of the roses she knew they were more than a gift. The fragrant arrangement signified the approval of Alessandro's father, and that mattered to her more than any one of the fabulous wedding presents that had arrived at the palace.

She could not remember ever feeling so keenly aware…so alive. And as she steadied herself for the walk up the aisle she found she could identify each strand of scent—incense, the roses resting in her arms, and the heady mix of countless exclusive perfumes. And above all the dazzling sights and sounds and scents, even though she never looked directly at him once, she was aware of Alessandro, waiting in silence for her at the end of the vast sweep of aisle.

Moving forward, Emily felt the burden of her long train ease as the squad of young train-bearers, chosen from schools in Ferara at her own request, took up the weight. And after a few brief moments of adjustment, when she feared she might lose the priceless tiara as the veil was tugged this way and that, they managed to keep pace with her perfectly.

She walked tall and proud at her father's side between the massed ranks of European royalty, wearing the slim column of a gown she had insisted upon. Only the splendour of the diamond tiara denoted her rank—that, and the floating pearl-strewn veil that eddied around her like a creamy-white mist. The only real colour was in her cheeks and in the coral-tinted roses her old friend had provided—Christopher Marlowe roses from the palace gardens, with every thorn removed, simply arranged and tied with silk ribbons in the colours of her new country: crimson, blue and gold.

She was aware of her mother in deep blue velvet, and Miranda, ravishing in palest lemon, as well as some other bridesmaids whom she had met only briefly. And then, as the organ sounded a fanfare of celebration, Emily focussed on the long walk ahead of her—the walk to join Alessandro, who stood waiting for her at the foot of the steps to the high altar.

The aisle itself was a work of art, paved in marble and carved by long-dead artisans to such effect that the scenes portrayed appeared more like faded photographs scanned onto the cool surface rather than the painstaking work of supreme craftsmen.

In front of her a vast window of such intense blue it appeared to be backlit by a power even greater than the sun threw splashes of colour across the faces of the dignitaries, some of whom Emily recognised, but she only sensed rather than saw every head turn her way, because her own gaze had found Alessandro's.

Even though she knew he was entering into marriage with no thought of love or romance, his strength lent her courage, and, seeing a flicker of concern in the eyes of his father, when Emily dropped her curtsey in front of him she smiled reassuringly as he reached forward to bring her to her feet.

Then she was standing next to Alessandro, with every fibre of her being pulsing with awareness… Alessandro, who appeared a daunting figure even in such a setting, where the scale of the building challenged normal perception. She matched her breathing to his, steadying herself, willing herself free of expectation, knowing that if she harboured none she could never be hurt.

But as the ceremony reached its climax a heady sense of destiny overcame her. Too much incense, she told herself firmly. But, whatever happened, she would do her best for the people of Ferara during her tenure as their Princess.

'You may kiss your bride.'

Reality struck home like a real physical blow. Would he kiss her? Or would he humiliate her in front of everyone? Was this hard for him? Impossible?

Too churned up to interpret anything, let alone the expression in her husband's eyes, Emily tensed as she waited. She didn't know what to expect.

He smiled, as if he was trying to imbue her with some of his own confidence. Alessandro, always considerate… thanking her for keeping her part of the bargain, Emily reasoned, wishing against her better judgement that it could be more. She felt his firm lips touch her mouth, pressing against the soft yielding pillow of her lips as she sighed against him—then a chord from the organ broke the spell and he linked her arm firmly through his.

And they were walking down the aisle together, man and wife, smiling to the left, and then smiling to the right—but never once smiling at each other.

They had their first row on their wedding night.

Elevated to a magnificent suite of rooms adjoining Alessandro's own, Emily prepared for bed alone. Her head was ringing with the effort of maintaining a front for so long. But at least she could console herself with the knowledge that she had begun to fulfil the requirements of their contract.

Who was she trying to kid? Emily wondered angrily as she sat down in front of the gilt-embossed dressing table mirror. A ceremony couldn't plug the chasm in her heart, or blot out her certainty that everything she had planned—so carefully, so meticulously—was already falling apart around her ears because she had made the classic mistake of allowing feelings to get in the way.

The fact that Alessandro was a prince didn't matter at

all—the fact that they had a business contract between them rather than a love affair mattered more to her than she could ever have imagined. It hurt like hell, she realised wistfully.

Plucking out the last of the pins holding her hair in place, she allowed it to spill over her shoulders and began to brush it with long, impassioned sweeps.

It was hard to believe she had been naïve enough to think she could simply pick up the pieces of her carefree single life and transfer them to Ferara with the rest of her luggage. Naïve? Her naïvety had been monumental, Emily thought, shaking her head angrily and then tossing the brush aside.

The wedding changed everything she realised, remembering the solemn vows she had made. Alessandro was her husband now, and she was his wife. And with those simple facts came hope, desire, expectation—and, most pressing of all, she thought, ramming her lips together as she tried not to cry, was the need to spend at least your wedding night with your husband.

Once they'd left the cathedral there had hardly been a chance for her to speak to him. And even when they had opened the reception by dancing together there had been constant interruptions. And she hadn't helped matters, Emily thought, remembering how stiffly she had held herself. There had been a moment when the toasts were made— Alessandro's hand had closed over her own as they'd sliced through a tier of the wedding cake and she had felt her whole body rebel and strain towards him. But she had clenched her fist over the handle until her knuckles had turned white and hurt…and apart from that—

She started at the knock on the door.

She had sent everyone away, taking the chance, once she had showered, to slip into a clean old top that had somehow found its way into the bottom of her suitcase. It didn't matter what she looked like. It could only be the maid with some hot milk, she reasoned, hurrying to the door.

'Alessandro!'

She felt foolish, standing there with bare feet, wearing nothing except an old faded top while her husband looked every bit as resplendent in a simple black silk robe as he had in full dress uniform, with medals and sash of office.

'I just came to see if you were all right…if you had everything you need,' he said, appearing not to register her choice of clothes as he scanned her sumptuous quarters as if running a mental inventory.

'I'm fine,' Emily replied. 'Just a little tired.'

'You looked beautiful today.' As he turned to look at her his gaze was steady and warm. 'Thank you, Emily.'

'It was nothing,' she lied, forcing a smile. But her glance strayed to his mouth as she remembered his kiss at the culmination of their marriage ceremony…chaste and dutiful maybe, but it still possessed the power to thrill her like no other kiss could ever hope to again. Recklessly she relived it now, briefly, self-indulgently, closing her eyes for just an instant as faint echoes of sensation shimmered through her frame.

'I think it all went well,' Alessandro said, breaking into her reverie.

'Yes,' she managed tightly. 'It all went very well. Miranda is in seventh heaven. The violin is everything—'

'Can we talk about us for a moment?'

His expression was hidden in shadow as he moved away from her towards one of the heavily draped windows, but Emily knew something had upset him. Perhaps he thought the violin too high a price to pay for a woman for whom he felt nothing.

'There's no reason why it should be awkward between us—' he began.

Awkward between them! What the hell was he talking about? Alessandro thought angrily, balling his hands into fists while in his mind the image of some rare bloom overlaid the fever. He swung around to look at her. Petals bruised easily, too easily—

'Are you all right?' Emily said, reaching out a hand. Then, remembering her position, she let it fall back again by her side.

He was completely naked under the robe; she was sure of it. Her speech had thickened as erotic possibilities crowded her mind... No one need ever know. They could be lovers and still end the contract as agreed. Just the possibility was a seduction in itself... The walls were twelve feet thick in this part of the old palace, she remembered. And their rooms were interconnecting. Most of the servants were still celebrating at one of the many parties in the palace grounds—she could still hear periodic explosions from the fireworks outside.

'I'm not aware of any awkwardness between us,' she said, in an attempt to prolong the conversation, trying not to stare too blatantly at the outline of his hard frame so clear in silhouette as he stood with his back to the window.

She was standing close to him now... close enough to detect the tang of the lemony soap he must have used in the shower. Closing her eyes, she inhaled deeply, then murmured dreamily, 'Don't worry, Alessandro. I'm completely at ease—'

She gasped in alarm as his fist hit the wall.

'"Don't worry, Alessandro"?' he mimicked softly, dangerously, and so close to her lips she could feel his warm breath on her face. 'How can you ask me not to worry? Am I the only one tense here? Don't lie to me, Emily,' he warned, pulling back. 'You're about as at ease with all this as I am.'

He took a couple of steps away, as if he couldn't bear to be close to her any more than she could bear to be parted from him.

'Please don't waste your breath on innocent protestations,' he said. 'I know you're lying to me. We're both in this over our heads, and you know it.'

'We knew what we were getting into—'

'Oh, did we?' He cut in sceptically. 'You're quite sure about that, are you, Emily? You're quite sure nothing's changed between us now that we're man and wife?'

He had taken the same mental journey she had, Emily realised with surprise. And each nuance in his voice betrayed the fact that he was every bit as disturbed by his thoughts as she was by her own.

'It's our wedding night—'

'So?' he demanded harshly.

'My no-sex clause—' She felt so foolish, so exposed. 'We could—'

'Forget it?' he suggested.

His gently mocking tone nudged her senses until she was unbearably aroused; the wet triangle of lace between her legs stretched taut in the struggle to contain her excitement.

'I don't think so, Emily,' he said harshly.

Every last remaining strand of common sense told her he was right, while her instinct, her desire, every hectic beat of her heart said she would stop at nothing to change his mind… But once the terms of their contract were satisfied he would need to move on, Emily reminded herself. Marry a woman of his own choosing—someone, as he had already intimated, who could shoulder the responsibilities of Ferara as an equal partner. There would be no place for her in Ferara then, so she would just have to find some way to rein in her hunger for that country's prince sooner rather than later.

Switching on the smile that had served her so well throughout the day, she agreed tonelessly that she did have everything she needed. But, just when she was complimenting herself on the cool way in which she'd handled the situation, Alessandro threw everything into confusion again.

'I suppose we could do as you suggest—keep the terms of our contract and yet have an affair,' he suggested bitterly.

There were a few moments of stunned silence, then Emily

laughed nervously—as if to show she knew he couldn't possibly be serious.

'What do you think, Emily?'

'What do I think?'

What *did* she think? She wasn't incapable of any thought, Emily realised as she watched him caress the door handle. Her belly ached with need for him. She was utterly beguiled by his strength, by the subtlety in his hands and by the strong, flexing power in his fingers… She wanted to know how all that would feel, transferred from hard steel to soft flesh—

'Well?' he said harshly.

Could he be serious? Her body seemed to think so.

Even as he watched her eyes darkening, and saw the tip of her tongue dart out to moisten her lips, Alessandro knew it wasn't enough. Even if Emily agreed, a sexual relationship with his beautiful new wife would only leave him more frustrated than ever. And he wanted more. He wanted much more. He wanted her love. He knew he had to do something…say something…or he might tip them both headlong into a situation from which neither of them would ever recover. He lifted his hands in a gesture of surrender.

'Forgive me, Emily. I don't know what I'm saying. I'm very tired—'

Yes, he was tired, Alessandro acknowledged. He was tired of all the play-acting, tired of pretending he didn't feel the most urgent need to consummate their marriage and ease the physical torment he was certain now that she felt every bit as much as he did. He longed to make Emily his wife, and in more than name only. He wanted them to be bound together, body and soul, for the rest of their lives.

But the weariness dragging at his mind had another cause, he accepted restlessly as he started to pace the room. What exhausted him the most was the secret he was forced to keep. The secret he bound so close because it was the one thing in the world that could take her away from him. And, in spite of the physical desire that raged through his body, he couldn't—he wouldn't—run the risk of losing her.

'We're both tired—and no wonder,' Emily observed gently, trying to hold her husband still from his angry pacing when she knew she had little more to soothe him with than her voice.

'I know,' Alessandro said, shaking his head as he stopped dead to look at her, as if for the first time. It was as if she understood everything…and nothing, he realised, passing a single finger down the side of her face. But it wasn't her fault…none of it was her fault.

Emily longed to grab hold of his hand then, and kiss it, and hold it against her cheek to warm him with her strength…her love… But the moment had passed, and now he was tense again. She could feel it in the air without looking at him.

'My behaviour just now was unforgivable,' Alessandro said, moving away from her. 'I'm sorry if I frightened you. The last thing I want is to make this any harder for you than it already is.' Reaching the door, he turned to face her again. 'Is there anything…anything at all, Emily…that I could provide for you here in Ferara to make you happy?'

'I am happy,' she protested quickly.

'Don't give me a glib answer because that's what you think I want to hear,' he warned. Leaning back against the door, he said softly, 'I mean it, Emily. Whatever you want—whatever it takes to make you happy—just name it.'

You, she thought, meeting his gaze steadily. That's all I want…you. First, last and always.

'You mentioned an idea for upgrading the palace apartments for staff—we could set up weekly meetings—'

'Yes,' she said quickly. Even a regular business meeting with him would be better than nothing at all. 'I think that's a wonderful idea.'

'I'm pleased you think so.'

Emily returned his smile. The first real smile she had seen on his face all day. But if he'd wanted her half as much as she wanted him they would have been setting up a very different sort of assignation, she reminded herself sadly.

One thing was sure: he wouldn't have been leaving her to spend their wedding night alone.

CHAPTER SEVEN

ALESSANDRO'S father sat up in bed to stare at his son in tolerant mystification.

'You come to my rooms at dawn to ask an old man like me what to do about the state of your marriage? Is this really my son Alessandro talking? I would hardly have believed it possible—before Emily came into your life,' he added, shaking his head. 'And had it not been for the nonsense you have told me about this—*contract*—' he spat out the word '—had it not been for that misplaced kindness to me, you would never have found yourself in this mess in the first place. How could you do such a thing, Alessandro? And how could you imagine such a travesty would work?'

I did it for you, Father…only for you, Alessandro thought, taking the rebuke in silence. And in spite of everything he couldn't find it in his heart to regret a thing…except that by trying to help his father it seemed that he had only succeeded in causing him more pain.

'Emily is like a tender bud—'

'I know, Father! I know!' Alessandro exclaimed impatiently, swiping the back of his neck with his hand as he sprang to his feet to pace the room like a tiger with a thorn in its pad. 'She is like no other woman I have ever met,' he went on, shaking his head in utter incomprehension. 'She shows no real interest in the priceless jewels she is entitled to wear, or the designer clothes I arranged to please her. She chooses instead to devote herself to the needs of our country, and to the small improvements she can make here at the palace. These…these are her passions.'

'Are you complaining, Alessandro?'

'No, Father! No. It's just that I am having to learn a whole new way of dealing with a woman. I feel like a youth embarking on his first love affair—'

'Perhaps this *is* your first love affair,' the old Prince murmured sagely.

'So, help me, Father. Tell me what to do.' Alessandro stopped, and levelled a blazing stare on his father's face. 'You must help me. Before I lose her.'

'You know what to do,' his father told him calmly. 'You know in your heart what is right, Alessandro. And if you want to make *me* happy, you will forget all about this foolish contract. Make this marriage work, Alessandro, or spend the rest of your life wishing that you had. It's up to you.'

Alessandro stopped pacing and stared unseeing into the distance. 'Monte Volere,' he murmured to himself. 'I shall take her to Monte Volere.' Then he turned around. 'Monte Volere, Father!'

'September…harvest-time in Monte Volere,' his father commented thoughtfully. 'A very good place to recharge the batteries of the heart.'

Alessandro felt the tension leave him as he watched a smile of contentment curl around his father's mouth.

'I think you've redeemed yourself, Alessandro. It's an excellent idea,' the old Prince declared with satisfaction.

'How soon can you be ready to leave?'

'Leave?' Emily said, still reeling from being shaken out of her slumbers by an Alessandro she had never seen before— black jeans, black tight-fitting top, black leather jacket slung across the broad sweep of his shoulders, tousled hair and yesterday's beard throwing shadows across the harsh planes of his handsome face.

But they were man and wife now, and her husband seemed to need her. 'Is everything all right?' she asked, instantly alert. 'Is it your father? Has something happened?'

'Yes. No. And, no—not yet,' he said, warming to her concern. 'My father's fine; don't worry.'

Alessandro was all tension and energy, like a coiled spring about to unwind—fast, Emily realised. 'So…?' she began curiously.

'How long?' Alessandro repeated, not troubling to hide his impatience now.

'Er…not long,' Emily admitted. 'I'd have to shower and—' She broke off uncertainly. 'Do I need to pack anything? Bring anything with me?' she elaborated, drawing up the sheet when the intimacy of his stare brushed something savage in both of them.

'You can shower when we get there. Come as you are.'

'In my nightclothes?'

'Why not?'

'Because it might cause a scandal?' Emily ventured cautiously.

Alessandro's look suggested that throwing her over his shoulder and storming off might cause a far bigger one.

'You're probably right,' he conceded reluctantly. 'So be quick. Just sling on your jeans and let's go.'

Jumping out of bed, Emily tore into her dressing room and, reaching into the very back of the wardrobe, where she had managed to conceal them from the army of wardrobe mistresses who had taken control of her clothes, she pulled out her jeans.

But the position of Princess came with conditions attached. One of the most onerous was that her appearance should never give cause for gossip or alarm. Discounting the crumpled denims out of hand, she grabbed a smart pair of navy trousers and a short-sleeved white blouse. They would do, Emily decided, gathering up her hair and securing it with a band and a couple of clips.

'Ready?' Alessandro said, barely looking at her as he grabbed hold of her forearm and dragged her with him.

'Ready,' Emily said, trying to catch her breath as she settled back in the passenger seat of a flame-red Ferrari.

'Good,' Alessandro said, narrowing his eyes as he concentrated on the road, his foot flat to the floor.

With the palace disappearing into the distance behind them, Emily was relieved to find Alessandro's driving fast but a good deal smoother than his chauffeur's. He drove without speaking, and finally, when she was almost bursting with curiosity, he announced that they would be stopping for lunch at a small village in the hills.

The Prince of Ferara's arrival with his new wife at an unpretentious café in the main square caused disbelief, followed swiftly by purposeful activity. And that was thanks largely to Alessandro's manner, Emily realised as she watched him putting people at their ease. He had barely finished introducing her around—and giving a pretty good impersonation of being proud of his choice of wife—when several women emerged from the kitchen, bearing local delicacies which they placed on the freshly scrubbed outdoor tables.

'You will need your strength,' one of them informed Alessandro coyly, nodding encouragement as she held out one of the first large oval dishes of pasta for him to taste.

'My strength?' he queried, making a point of not looking at Emily, though she noticed the smile he was gracious enough to hide behind a huge red-chequered napkin.

'*Si*, Principe,' all the other women chorused gaily, much to Emily's embarrassment.

Then one of the men threaded his way through the women, flexing a battered cap in his hand. 'Today is the Palio del Timone, Principe,' he explained. 'Each year we have a tug o' war with the neighbouring village; you have arrived just in time—' He stopped, as if he felt he had gone too far.

'Go on,' Alessandro encouraged, putting down his fork to listen.

'If you took part…' The man hesitated again.

Alessandro got to his feet and clapped him on the shoulder. 'Of course I will take part.'

'Federico,' the man supplied, flashing up an expectant glance.

'Federico,' Alessandro said, shaking him by the hand, 'you have just recruited a new member to your team. I am honoured to serve with you.'

Rubbing his hands together with glee, Federico turned. 'Did you hear that? I believe this year we may just have the edge!'

As the excitement rose to fever-pitch, Emily remembered Alessandro had been in a rush when they left the palace. 'Are you sure there's time for this?' she murmured with concern as she joined him.

'Why not?' he demanded, looking at her in amusement. 'How much of a hurry are you in, Principessa?'

As she went after him Emily's face was bright red, provoking delighted smiles and knowing looks from those women close enough to observe the exchange.

If their marriage had been consummated, Emily reckoned, a little embarrassment would have been a small price to pay. But as it was it seemed particularly unjust—especially as the women were still nudging each other and winking at her.

The news that Alessandro was to take part in the competition had spread like wildfire, and it seemed as if the entire population of the village had managed to crowd themselves into the small paved area around the café. Silence fell as he crossed the square to greet the opposing team. It was obvious that his side was at a considerable disadvantage, as most were older than their rowdy young opponents from the neighbouring village.

'Do you think you can redress the balance?' Emily asked anxiously, as she watched him strip to the waist. His naked torso was all the answer she needed, and a murmur of approval rose around them as he handed her the black top.

'Take up the slack,' the man from the café ordered, pointing to the thick rope lying on the ground. 'Principessa,' he added, 'when you drop the flag, the men must put their weight and their strength behind that rope. The first team to haul the others across that white line wins the Palio.'

Emily tried to concentrate—but was there anything more delicious than seeing Alessandro put his weight and his strength behind that rope? she wondered, watching the flex of muscles on his sun-bronzed body. If there was, she could only imagine it would be Alessandro completely stripped of his clothes.

His glance flashed across at precisely that moment, filling Emily with a very different kind of excitement from the rest of the spectators. And as she dropped the flag he gave a slight smile that seemed to promise her a contest no less involving than the one he was embarking upon.

Emily watched the denim mould around his impressive thighs as he dug his heels into the ground, gravel spitting up either side of his feet as he heaved. Each muscle and sinew was clearly defined as he threw every bit of his strength behind the rope, working to drag the other side closer to the line.

It was all over very suddenly. A groan from the losing side and a triumphant shout from Alessandro's who, brandishing the rope, punched the air with their fists. Then there was a noisy round of back-slapping and congratulations, as well as good-natured banter before Alessandro came back to reclaim his top.

'I'll just take a shower, then I'll be right with you,' he promised, wheeling away to accompany Federico. 'Then we'll go,' he called back to her over his shoulder. 'Be ready.'

The villagers wanted Alessandro to share in their celebrations, and were disappointed when he told them he had to leave. But, having exacted a promise from him to return the following year, they accepted his decision and fell back.

'If we are to reach Monte Volere before bedtime, I must go now,' he explained, provoking another round of nudges and tempting Emily to disillusion everyone on the spot. Her husband's hair might have been still wet from the shower, and his top clinging damply to the water droplets around his neck—giving the impression that he was in such a hurry to get back to her he hadn't troubled to dry himself properly—but she knew he only wanted to get to his country estate before dark.

Beyond the narrow streets and close-clustered village houses the countryside opened into a vast, sprawling plain. As the tawny volcanic soil paled to blonde they sped on through the pale, freshly tilled earth on an arrow-straight road, until another range of hills, even higher than those they had left behind, loomed in front of them.

'Not long now,' Alessandro promised as he began to negotiate a series of tortuous hairpin bends. 'I'm going to stop when we get to the top,' he informed her. 'Then you'll see one of the most spectacular vistas in all of Ferara.'

Emily formed a sound of appreciation in her throat. But the last thing on her mind after the events in the village was a sightseeing trip. And even if Alessandro's suggestion of an affair between them had been his idea of a joke, she had believed this trip to his country estate signalled his intention to bring them closer—if only for the sake of appearances. Now she knew the visit was nothing more than proof he intended to keep his word and show her around. And, keen as she was to learn more about Ferara, she was keener still to learn more about her husband.

'Save it,' she muttered ungraciously.

As Alessandro shot her a curious glance Emily regretted

the outburst. He was only doing what he thought was right—what he thought she would enjoy.

'No. I insist,' he said firmly.

She had to admit he was right about the view. As she climbed out of the car Emily felt like an eagle staring down at the lake, tiny below them, shimmering in the heat haze like a panel of jewel-encrusted silk.

'It's absolutely stunning,' she murmured, fighting off the insane urge to move close enough to slip her arm through his.

'This region of Ferara has many similarities to the fiords of Norway,' Alessandro said. 'Don't stand too close to the edge,' he warned, coming to stand between Emily and the sheer drop only a metre or so in front of her feet.

Emily smiled, then felt unaccountably bleak when he started back to the car as if there was some other fabulous camera opportunity waiting just around the next bend for them.

'You will find there is a lot of variety in Ferara,' Alessandro remarked as he turned the car back onto what was now little more than a steep mountain track. 'I hope you will eventually come to love it as much as I do.'

And the point would be…? Emily thought his remark strange, bearing in mind the peculiar circumstances of their marriage. 'Mmm,' she managed non-committally.

But if the view he had shown her had been the eagle's perch, then his estate at Monte Volere was the eagle's eyrie, she discovered as Alessandro turned in beneath a narrow stone archway. Set on the highest point of a hill cloaked with vineyards, the pink and cream stone of the old manor house glowed rose-red where shadows were painted by the failing light.

'Why have you brought me here?' she said curiously.

Alessandro turned to stare at her, an amused expression tugging at his mouth. 'Rest and recreation—'

'No. Really,' Emily insisted.

'Really,' Alessandro replied steadily as he drew to a halt in front of the old building. 'I thought you needed to get away from everything…everyone…for a few days.'

'To be alone?'

But Alessandro had already climbed out of the car.

'I'll show you to your room,' he called over his shoulder as she followed him up the steps. He opened an oak door and beckoned her inside.

My room? Emily thought, banishing the sense of disappointment. She stared across the stone-flagged hall as Alessandro sprinted up the stairs.

'Well?' he said, leaning over the carved wooden banister. 'Aren't you coming?'

The room he showed her into had been made cosy with throws, rugs and cushions in a variety of warm colours. One wall was almost completely devoted to a huge fireplace, carved from a single block of mellow honey-coloured sandstone. This housed a black wrought-iron grate and, because there was no need for a fire, an earthenware dish containing dried pot pourri to provide a splash of colour on the terracotta tiles. A wide-armed fan whirred lazily on the ceiling, stirring the scent of dried rose petals into the air. The thin coating of yellow ochre paint on the rough plaster walls had paled to lemon where the sunlight had faded it over many years, and exposed oak beams supported the high, sloping ceiling over the vast four-poster bed. Dressed with crisp white bedlinen, this offered a breathtaking view over the surrounding countryside—something Emily discovered when impulsively she flung herself down on it and bounced up and down.

'I'll be right across the landing if you need me,' Alessandro said, closing the door quietly behind him before she had a chance to say a word.

Suddenly Monte Volere didn't seem so appealing—she didn't even want to be there any more. Gusting a long, shaky sigh, Emily stared around the empty room. If this was

Alessandro's idea of a honeymoon— She mashed her lips together, remembering he wasn't much good at wedding nights either. But she wouldn't let it get her down. No expectations, no disappointments, she reminded herself—and at least the bed looked comfy.

As Emily had anticipated, the high bed was extremely comfortable. The ceiling fan turned rhythmically over her head, soothing her while it kept everything airily pleasant. Over and above all this, she had taken a leisurely bath to ensure she got a good night's sleep—but, glancing at the clock, she saw it was three o' clock in the morning.

Safe to say success has *not* crowned my ventures, she thought, staring across at the closed door onto the landing. Irrationally, she felt an overwhelming urge to open it. Open it, and then what? Emily asked herself impatiently, giving her pillows an extra thump. And then leave the rest to fate, she decided, after another period of restless thrashing. Swinging her feet onto the cool tiled floor, she padded silently across the room. With care, she managed to lift the heavy wrought-iron latch without making a sound. Cautiously, she tested the door. The hinges were well oiled, and the movement was squeak-free. Opening it a little more, so that it looked like an invitation rather than an oversight, she hurried back to bed with her heart thundering in anticipation.

Above the sound of the fan she thought she could hear something…footsteps, maybe—measured, rhythmical—pacing, she decided. It had to be Alessandro, since he had already told her that the staff at Monte Volere came in on a daily basis, so she knew they were all alone in the house.

Arranging herself on the pillows, Emily fluffed out her long hair, moistened her lips, listened—and waited.

Across the landing Alessandro, after tossing and turning all night, found himself pacing the floor like a pent-up warrior on the eve of battle. Emerging from his angry introspection for a few moments, he noticed Emily's door open. Feeling sure that he had closed it behind him earlier in the evening, he felt a rush of concern for her. Pulling on his jeans, he crossed his room to investigate.

Leaning against the wall just outside his bedroom, he paused, consciously stilled his breathing, and listened. They were still alone in the house; he was sure of it. The only noises he could detect were the typical muted creaks and groans of old timber as it cooled and relaxed after the heat of the day.

But, just to make absolutely certain Emily was safe, he crossed the landing, taking care to move silently, and stared into her room.

With her senses on full alert Emily detected the movement even though she heard nothing. Licking her lips one last time, she closed her eyes and concentrated on taking deep, calming breaths. Her limbs felt deliciously suspended and a seductive lethargy rolled over her…her nerve-endings grew increasingly sensitive as she lay still and contemplated Alessandro's imminent arrival.

Emily…his wife, Alessandro mused, incredulous that it was so as he gazed at her still figure. Could it be possible that she was even more beautiful asleep than awake? Then, remembering the strength of character that burned in her eyes, and the firm set of her mouth whenever she was angry with him, he smiled and shook his head in a quick gesture of denial. And she was lovelier still when she smiled, he remembered. And when she laughed…

His gaze lingered on her mouth. The temptation to cross the room, to match his length to hers and to tease open those full, sensuous lips…lips he was sure waited like the rest of her to be awakened—

He stopped himself. The open door was her protection, he realised. How could he surprise her when she was beginning at last to trust him? He could not take advantage of the open door. He would not frighten her by entering the room when she was asleep. Spinning around, he returned to his own room after making sure that his wife's bedroom door was closed securely behind him.

Breakfast was a tense affair. Cursing herself for behaving like a lovesick fool, Emily accepted that she had received no more than she deserved…which was precisely nothing.

Alessandro seemed cool and distant, though as polite as ever. Dismissing the cook who had come in to prepare the food for them, he insisted on waiting on her himself at breakfast.

'This really is far too much for me,' Emily protested, when he handed her a dish piled high with freshly peeled and sliced peaches, and a second plate covered in a selection of cold meats and cheeses.

'Eat,' he commanded impatiently, returning to the table where their breakfast buffet had been laid out only to return with some warm bread rolls. 'You'll need your strength today.'

'Need my strength?' Emily said suspiciously. 'For what?'

'We've got a busy day ahead of us.'

Watching him tear into his own roll, and stab at a plate of cheese with the energy of ten, Emily felt her spirits take a dive. Hiking, she guessed—at the very least. Mountaineering, probably—both of which filled her with dread. 'You mean a day of physical activities?'

'Mmm,' Alessandro confirmed gruffly, his eyes glittering with a dangerous light. Draining his coffee cup fast, he pushed it away. 'Grape-treading,' he rapped purposefully.

'Grape-treading?' Emily echoed, following him with her eyes as he strode to view the massed fields of vines through the open window. The occasion was sure to be fascinating to watch, she thought. Her glance embraced Alessandro's powerful forearms and the broad sweep of his chest. What part would he play in the proceedings? she wondered, hoping it would require him to strip to the waist again.

'What?' he demanded, thrusting his fingers into the back pockets of his jeans as he turned around. 'What are you staring at?' he repeated, more insistently.

Emily tore her gaze away from the well-muscled thighs so tantalisingly defined in snug-fitting denim. 'Nothing,' she said dismissively, with a flip of her hand. 'I'd like that very much. For you to take me to the grape-treading, I mean.'

'Good.'

That voice again, she realised, turning her face away so that he couldn't see her reddening under his calculating and extremely disturbing gaze. 'I had no idea that such archaic practices survived,' she said, rustling up her most professional manner.

'Just about everything is mechanised these days.' Alessandro said, accommodating her approach. 'But for the highest quality wines only an experienced eye can judge the grapes. So we keep our vines low and pick by hand. It is hard work, and must be completed quickly before the heat of the sun raises acidity levels.'

She tensed as he prowled closer. 'I see…'

'Oh, do you?' he murmured sardonically, somewhere very close to her ear.

'But surely you can't tread all those grapes out there?' she said edgily, staring fixedly out of the window as she waited for her face to cool down.

'Of course not, ' Alessandro said, standing right beside her. 'The grape-treading is purely symbolic. It marks the start of the harvest.'

He refused to take the hint as she moved away, and suddenly was right in front of her again.

Glancing from side to side, Emily realised she was boxed into a corner between an old oak dresser and a bookcase. How on earth had that happened? she wondered, sagging with relief when he moved away.

'Different varieties of grape ripen at different times,' he continued evenly, as if their game of tag, at which he was clearly a master, had never taken place. 'And when they are all safely gathered in we celebrate, with a proper Festa del Villaggio. The custom of treading some of the grapes the old way after the first picking is said to placate the forces of nature.'

Emily began to relax. The history of the grape was surprisingly interesting…or perhaps it was more relief that, having distracted them both by explaining it, Alessandro was allowing the sexual tension between them to ease. She inclined her head to demonstrate her fascination with the subject, hoping her body would take the hint and calm down, too.

'It is also carried out to ensure good weather,' Alessandro went on, in the same soothing tone. Without any warning, he crossed the room, seized her arms, and held her close. 'So, Emily,' he demanded impatiently, 'will you come?'

'I'd love to.' After all, she persuaded herself as his hands relaxed, the chance to get to know her husband a little better, to see him interacting with the villagers, was an opportunity that might never come again.

'Great. You'll have to get changed first.'

'You mean it's today—right now?' She should have guessed! 'Why can't I go like this?'

'Well, if you want to look like you're heading for court—'

'Without a jacket—?' As she pulled a face his lips tugged up in a half-smile. 'You're teasing me.'

'Am I?' he murmured provocatively.

'OK, so now what? Point me in the direction of the nearest shops?' Emily demanded, confronting Alessandro, hands on hips when he started laughing. 'Please, Alessandro. Don't be difficult. I want to go with you. Just tell me where the shops are and I'll go and buy something suitable to wear.'

'OK. I'll take you.'

'Thank you,' Emily said graciously.

'We can walk there,' he said, when she stopped at the passenger door of the four-wheel drive he'd told her he used to get about the estate.

'Walk?' Emily couldn't imagine how she had missed a dress shop as they drove through.

'Certainly,' Alessandro said, striding away in the direction of the fields. 'It will only take ten minutes or so to reach Maria Felsina's cottage.

'Cottage?' Emily demanded, increasing to a trot to keep up.

'You'll see. Come on,' he urged, speeding up again. 'We haven't got all day. You don't want the grape-treading to start without us, do you?' he called over his shoulder.

A suspicion had taken root in Emily's mind. 'You mean we'll actually be taking part?'

Alessandro's loafers slapped rhythmically against the hard-baked earth. 'Of course,' he called back. 'Why else would we be going?'

'I don't know…I'm not—'

'Not what?' Alessandro demanded impatiently. He blazed a stare at her. 'Do you want to come with me?'

'Of course I do. But—'

Taking her arm in a firm grip, Alessandro marched on in silence.

As they stood in front of the modest dwelling, waiting for the door to open, Emily still felt bemused at the possibility of shopping for clothes inside such a tiny cottage.

'Don't look so worried,' Alessandro said as he turned to look down at her. 'Maria will find you something to wear.'

Emily made a conscious effort to relax. 'I'm fine,' she said.

All the signs of a much loved home surrounded them. There wasn't a single weed to be seen in the garden, and the colourful flowerbeds to either side of the newly swept path were crammed with blooms. The shuttered windows beside the front door were underscored with planters overflowing with blossom, while heavily scented climbers jostled for space around the doorframe.

Closing her eyes, Emily tried to concentrate on the sounds of the bees buzzing and the birdsong; the mingled perfume of flowers, all so delightful and distinctive. Had she been alone, she might have succeeded. But Alessandro was standing very close, claiming every bit of her notice—and why was he making such a fuss about kitting her out for the grape-treading? Surely she would only need to roll up her trouser-legs and don some sort of overall—?

She came to full attention as the door swung open. A short, generously proportioned woman, as creased and as brown as a walnut, slapped her hands together when she saw Alessandro and cried out with pleasure, 'Alessandro! *Piccolino!*'

'My nanny,' Alessandro explained, swinging the old lady off the ground with an answering shout.

Emily watched as a frantic exchange of questions and answers ensued between them.

'Maria apologises for being at the end of the garden tending her geese,' Alessandro translated. 'Her favourite, Carlotta, is to take part in the annual goose race and must have extra care. True,' he assured Emily when he saw the look on her face. 'One day I'll take you to see the race. These birds are treated like favoured members of the family. And the winner…' He gave a low whistle of appreciation.

'Fed to the family?' Emily guessed wryly.

'Certainly not!' Alessandro said with a grin. 'There is a substantial cash prize at stake—to keep the winning goose in luxury for the rest of its life. It is up to the owner to ensure that this is the case. A matter of honour,' he explained, pinning a serious expression on his face. 'And now Maria invites us into her home.'

'*Si,*' Signora Felsina insisted, nodding her head enthusiastically as she beamed at Emily.

Stepping over the stone threshold, Emily looked around curiously. The tiny cottage windows allowed in little natural light, but several old-fashioned oil lamps had been lit so that everything was softly illuminated. She could smell something delicious cooking on the old black range, and noticed that the best use had been made of the narrow window ledges, which housed an array of pungent green herbs flourishing in terracotta pots.

Contentment was contagious, she discovered, hoping they could stay for a little while. Everything was ordered for comfort. Every object had been arranged to please the eye. And all of it gleamed with the unmistakable patina of regular attention. A bolt of desire pierced her heart as she glanced across at Alessandro—desire that went way beyond the physical to claw at her soul. Did he feel it, too? Did he long for a sanctuary like this to call his own? Could he feel the tug of a real home? The longing to create a similar haven was overwhelming her—

'Sit, Principessa, sit—'

The heavily accented voice of the older woman interrupted Emily's reveries.

'Here,' she insisted, tossing rugs and cushions aside. 'Sit here, Principessa.'

'Emily. Please…call me Emily.'

Something in Emily's voice must have troubled the older woman. Her hand lingered on Emily's arm as she turned to confront Alessandro.

'Alessandro,' she said, her voice mildly chastening. 'Your bride is not happy. What is wrong, Alessandro?'

Emily tensed at the bluntness of the remark, but Alessandro seemed not to have taken offence.

At his non-committal grunt Maria shook her head, and took herself off to pour out three fizzing glasses of homemade ginger beer from a vast stone flagon. 'You sit, too,' she said, turning around to face Alessandro. 'You take up too much space,' she complained fondly as she transferred the squat glasses onto a wooden tray.

'Here, let me,' he said, ignoring her instruction and removing the tray from her hands. 'Now, *you* go and sit down, *tata*.'

Emily watched as the old lady hurried to obey his instruction, noticing her beam of delight when Alessandro used what surely must have been his childhood name for her.

Settling herself down into a chair so plumped up with cushions her chubby sandal-clad feet barely touched the ground, Maria Felsina held her glass aloft as she made a smiling toast to Emily.

'Emily,' Alessandro echoed softly.

Draining her glass with relish, Maria leaped to her feet and declared, 'And now you must eat—'

'Oh, no—' Emily protested. She was still full from breakfast, but Alessandro's glance warned her to stay silent. 'Thank you,' she said, seeing she might cause offence by refusing one of the sugar-frosted buns. 'These look delicious.' And they were, she realised, as the moist, feather-light sponge slipped down her throat.

In spite of the warm late-summer weather, there was a low fire in the grate, and as she ate Emily longed to open some buttons at the neck of her tailored shirt. She went so far as to toy with the top one—but when Alessandro caught her glance for some reason, the innocent action suddenly struck her as irredeemably provocative. She looked away, but not before she saw one of his sweeping raven brows rise minutely in an expression that was both accusing and amused.

'My wife has come to you for clothes, *tata*,' he said, turning his attention back to his old nurse.

'Will they fit?' Emily murmured discreetly.

Alessandro must have translated this, Emily thought, judging by their peals of laughter. Before she could feel embarrassed, Maria took her hand and stroked it gently, as if to atone for the outburst. Then, confirming Emily's reading of the situation, she turned a face full of mock reproach on Alessandro and wagged a blunt-nailed finger at him.

'Maria is the best dressmaker on the estate,' Alessandro explained. 'She'll soon sort you out with something to wear.'

'In time?' Emily said anxiously.

Her concern crossed the language barrier, and with a vigorous nod of her head Maria indicated that she should follow her into the next room. Taking her through a low door, Maria pointed to some bolts of cloth stacked in one corner of the room, and then at the old treadle sewing machine standing against the wall.

There was a makeshift gown-rail—just a piece of rope suspended between two hooks on a low joist—and crammed onto this were cotton skirts in a startling profusion of colour and pattern, together with white puff-sleeved tops, all with the same scooped necks and tie fronts.

'*Ecco*, Principessa!' Maria exclaimed. And then, after viewing her thoughtfully for few moments, Maria swooped on the rail and unhooked an armful of clothing.

'Oh, no! I couldn't possibly!' Emily protested, seeing the top was so low her belly button would get an airing, never mind anything else. When Maria pressed it into her hands she bundled it behind her back, hoping Alessandro, who had just appeared at the door, hadn't noticed.

His eyes sparkled dangerously in the dim light. 'Well? Go and try them on,' he urged softly.

'Will you—?'

'I'll come back when you're changed,' he said reassuringly.

Next, Maria held out a selection of skirts for her to choose from, and Emily surprised herself by selecting the gaudiest one.

Maria smiled, nodding approval of her choice, shaking out the fabric equivalent of a sunset.

The prospect of wearing something so showy...so decadent...was exciting. Pulling on the skirt, Emily began to do battle with the blouse, managing at last to adjust the front into something approaching respectability.

'No, no,' Maria protested, waggling her finger. 'Like this, Principessa,' she said, with a broad grin on her face.

Before Emily could stop her Maria had tugged the elasticated top below her shoulders until there was more cleavage on show than ever. But the older woman still wasn't satisfied, and, plucking at Emily's bra strap, she shook her head in disapproval.

With a rueful laugh Emily finally capitulated and, reaching behind her back, freed the catches on her bra. As the last restraint was removed even she had to admit the result was impressive.

Indicating there was one last thing to be changed, Maria darted down to reach beneath an old wooden chest. Pulling out a pair of simple brown leather sandals, scarcely more than a thong to stick between the toes on strips of toughened leather, she pushed them across the stone-flagged floor towards Emily.

'Grazie,' Emily said, flashing up a smile as she slipped them on. They were surprisingly comfortable, she found, wiggling her toes and relishing the freedom. As she straightened up, Maria reached for the pins that were already finding it a struggle to contain Emily's heavy mane of shiny black hair. They were cast aside, and with a final flourish Maria carefully drew her fingers through the resulting cascade, arranging it like a gleaming cloak around her protégée's shoulders.

Standing back, she beamed with satisfaction and, taking hold of Emily's arm, turned her around to view her reflection in the mirror.

Even the short time she had been in the hot climate had warmed Emily's skin-tone to gold, and the brazen hussy staring back at her bore no resemblance whatever to the tight-laced professional she was accustomed to seeing. Instead, a full-breasted woman, with wild, untamed hair streaming across her shoulders, gazed back proudly. Toned legs, full lips, and dark up-tilted eyes suggested endless possibilities…endless fantasies…

As Maria gusted with approval Emily started to move towards the door. At the last moment she hesitated; dressing up, play-acting, was one thing, but her husband was all too real—and she didn't know him well enough to be able to predict how he would react when he saw his wife parading about like some fugitive from a bawdy etching. There was a distinct possibility she might unleash a whole lot more than she could cope with.

At the sound of a low, appreciative whistle she froze.

'That's quite an improvement.'

Leaning up against the doorframe, his arms loosely folded, Alessandro made no attempt to hide his interest in her newly adopted persona. 'You really look the part,' he murmured, giving Maria a wry nod of approval.

Raising her head defiantly, Emily stared him square in the eyes. What part was that? she wondered suspiciously.

'Leave the rest of your clothes here,' he said, straightening up. 'We'll pick them up later. Come on,' he pressed, 'everyone will be waiting for us.'

And, before she could refuse, he stretched out, caught hold of her, and swept her out of the door.

CHAPTER EIGHT

THEY were in a huge barn filled with the young men and women of the village. The contrast to the dappled light of the afternoon was apparent the moment Alessandro slid shut the huge wooden door behind them. Inside the barn Emily was conscious of a heady, sensuous quality to the heavy golden air that was lacking on the outside.

Ribbons of sunlight slanted across a sea of smiling faces, while the scent of young, clean bodies merged with the more pungent aroma of ripe fruit. There was an air of expectancy, and even sound seemed in thrall to the mellow mood, Emily discovered, when a murmur of welcome rose like a wave, subsided first to a whisper, and then to silence as Alessandro raised his hands.

She saw that here there was no protocol; her husband was greeted as warmly and as naturally as if he was just another man from the village, come to show off his new bride. His loud greeting was matched by the shouts of the other men present and then, turning to Emily, he urged her forward.

There was complete silence as everyone waited to see what she would do.

She felt her cheeks grow hot, and for a moment she held back. But the firm touch of Alessandro's hand on her arm gave her no choice and, stepping forward, she executed a smiling curtsey to the assembled crowd.

'Thank you,' Alessandro rasped, very close to her ear.

Emily turned and smiled back at him, the cheers resounding in her ears. She felt a warm rush of happiness to know that her action had pleased him.

She watched as he tugged his shirt over his head, and then saw that she wasn't the only woman looking at him with naked appreciation.

And some of the village girls weren't afraid to move closer. Instinctively, Emily moved onto the offensive. Almost before she knew what she was doing she had placed herself between Alessandro and his admirers.

As he toed off his shoes he saw what she was doing, and threw her a half-smile that rippled through her body with startling consequences.

Was it a challenge? Emily wondered, conscious that the other women had backed off. Keeping her eyes locked on Alessandro's, she kicked off her own sandals.

Matching her stare for stare, he leaned forward and rolled up the legs of his jeans.

Holding his gaze, Emily tossed back her hair, then, emulating all the other women, she picked up the hem of her skirt and secured it into her underwear. She had never been consciously proud of her legs before, but now she was—especially when Alessandro's eyes broke their hold on her own to lavish a lingering and frankly appreciative gaze on them.

He was naked apart from his jeans, and his hard, muscled torso gleamed like a priceless bronze in the sultry haze, setting him apart from all the other men. It wasn't simply the power in his body, Emily realised as their eyes locked again, or even his extra height. It was that bone-melting menace in his dark, angled stare.

Prowling the floor around her, it seemed almost as if it was now Alessandro's turn to draw an invisible barrier between Emily and the rest of the men, so that even amidst the crowd she was undeniably and unmistakably his.

Emily's breath caught in her throat. Involuntarily, she touched her tongue to her lips, and one of the young women, misreading her expression, took it for uncertainty. Leaving her partner on the outskirts of the crowd, she alone dared to breach the invisible circle her Prince had drawn around his wife.

Taking Emily by the arm, she drew her across the sawdust-covered floor towards the huge open vat that stood at one end of the barn. Leading her up the steps, she brought her onto the high platform of seasoned oak.

'Come,' she said softly, in lightly accented English. 'You must be the first to climb in, Principessa.'

A low murmur of approval rose from the men, then died the instant Alessandro shifted his position and started moving towards her.

'I'll lift you in,' he murmured, just as she was about to climb over the side.

Convincing herself that the only reason she would allow him to do that was because there were so many people watching and she couldn't refuse, Emily proudly inclined her head. There was something about the very special atmosphere surrounding them that made her acutely aware of the power of her femininity. It was a force she could use, or not, as she chose…

But she had overlooked the fact that she had not felt Alessandro's arms around her since they had danced together at their wedding reception. And now, thanks to her own reckless choice of clothes and the sensuous ambience in which they found themselves, she was intensely aroused.

The touch of his hands around her waist was electrifying. She closed her eyes and told herself not to read anything into it. But Alessandro took delight in lowering her as slowly as he could, so that it seemed to Emily as if a lifetime of pleasure was encapsulated in the few seconds it took to sink down into the mountain of grapes. The silence around them had thickened and taken on a new significance, as if everyone in the barn was holding a collective breath. As she sank lower she could feel the swollen fruit bursting beneath her feet, until her legs were completely submerged to the very top of her thighs.

When Alessandro vaulted over the side to join her a great cheer went up, temporarily diminishing the sensuous mood. It seemed his presence in the vat was the sign for everyone else to climb in, and a mad scramble ensued as tiny spaces were claimed; couples were so closely entwined it was impossible to see where one handsome youth ended and his pretty young partner began.

In the melee, Emily was thrust up tight against Alessandro, her feet struggling for purchase on the warm, slippery juice and split skins. She was forced to cling onto him just in order to remain standing. Relaxing gradually, as he steadied her, she became aware of his heart thrumming rhythmically against her breasts and his naked chest like warm marble beneath her hands.

The air was intoxicating, and stimulating, filled with the perfume of grapes and juice and heightened emotion. There was so much noise, so much covert—and not so covert— activity between the couples, that Emily felt shielded by it, free to indulge in her wildest fantasies, to become someone else altogether, someone far more daring and provocative than she could ever hope to be…

Then, as if at some silent signal, the noise stilled as suddenly as it had begun. Out of the silence rose a moistly slow and regular beat. It was impossible to ignore and useless to resist, and, after missing only a couple of the moves, Emily found herself joining in with the rest and stamping her feet in a rhythmical pattern.

As the pace increased the atmosphere became charged with a new and primal energy, and, clinging on to Alessandro, Emily felt her senses respond urgently. She softened against him, each of her muscles yielding in turn, until finally she was moulded into him, moving to his rhythm, their rhythm, to the insistent, unavoidable rhythm that consumed them both.

As she abandoned herself time stood still and meant nothing. She no longer knew where she began and he ended. The only certainty was that she was safe in his arms, and it was to his eyes that her overheated glance flew for approval.

Soon her clothes were drenched and she was coated all over with the sweet, sticky juice. She noticed that some of their companions were already beginning to peel away, clambering out over the sides of the vat in untidy, exhausted groups. She noticed too how a haze of passion seemed to linger behind each departure, hovering in the air around her and in the lingering exchange of slanted glances as couples retired silently into the shadows, arms intertwined and bodies fused in tense expectation.

Quite suddenly she was alone with Alessandro.

Leaning against the side of the great vat, his arms outstretched and resting lightly on the rim, he studied her calmly. Emily felt as if even the air she breathed was saturated with sensuality. She was trembling as he moved towards her, remained quiescent when he swept her into his arms, and felt bereft, even for those few moments of separation, after he had lowered her down over the side of the vat…

Vaulting over to join her, Alessandro twined his fingers through hers and drew her quickly down the steps with him, across the floor of the barn towards another door she hadn't noticed before. From there he took her across a small cobbled yard, made shady by a roof of densely intertwined grapevines, and, unlatching another door, he brought her inside the facing building, and shot home a sturdy black bolt.

They were locked in together, closed off completely from the outside world. Streamers of sunlight strung from the roof trusses high over their heads brightened the honey gold air humming around them, and as Alessandro mounted some open wooden steps with Emily in his arms she registered hazily that he was carrying her up to the hayloft.

Alessandro brought her to a mezzanine level, where the floor was hidden beneath a deep, soft carpet of sweet-smelling hay. Setting her down gently, he sat beside her and drew her onto his lap, stretching out his long legs as he eased back against the bales of hay.

Emily felt as if she might drown in his eyes, as if the depth of expression had been there all the time, waiting for her, if only she'd had the courage to see it. There were no divisions between them now, only the gasping, pleading murmurs escaping her lips that left Alessandro under no illusion as to how much she wanted him and how hard it was for her to wait.

Pausing only to snatch apart the grape-stained ties of her blouse, he dragged the fabric away and plunged his tongue between her breasts to lick the sticky juices off. Feasting on sweetness, his questing mouth found first one succulent extended nipple and then the next, while Emily, meshing her fingers through his hair, could only beg him not to stop.

'I have no intention of stopping, *cara mia*,' Alessandro husked, holding her firm beneath him. 'Not until every last drop of juice has been licked from your body.'

And as he moved back to his task Emily found her pleasure increased when she could watch her body responding to his touch. The sound of her own rapid breathing, coupled with the deeper, throaty sounds of contentment from Alessandro, added a piquancy to her enjoyment she could never have anticipated as he fulfilled his pledge with devastating thoroughness. And, in spite of her impatience, Alessandro continued to prepare her with the utmost care, as if he knew how inexperienced she was.

When at last his hands reached down to throw back her skirt, she thrust up her hips in desperate haste, willing to go to any lengths now to make it easier for him. But he broke away, swinging to his feet as he reached for the buckle on his belt. Then, dropping back to his knees by her side, he took her face between his warm hands and kissed her very slowly, so that she was in no doubt how deep his feelings ran.

'Don't be frightened,' he murmured, reaching to strip off the rest of his clothes.

Emily gave an involuntary gasp and looked away. Nothing could have prepared her for the sight of Alessandro naked, and aroused. 'No,' she gasped instinctively, pulling back.

'No?' he queried softly, reaching up inside her blouse. His slow, seductive strokes soothed her, and then he took each engorged nipple-tip between his fingers and tugged a little. Smiling down at her, he murmured, 'Are you quite sure about that, Emily?'

The only answer possible was a series of small gasps—gasps that became cries of delight as he replaced the touch of his hands with his mouth.

'Do you still want me to stop?' Alessandro taunted her softly, whispering the words against her neck, so that she shivered with pleasure and pressed against him all the more.

'No,' Emily moaned, wanting only his touch and his kisses, not his questions.

'Are you sure?'

She reassured him frantically with every persuasive phrase she could think of. He would be a wonderful lover, she was sure of it, and that certainty increased her desire for him until it filled her whole world.

'So, you're not scared of me now?' he pressed gently.

'Scared?' Emily scoffed faintly, turning her face away so that he could not see how brazen he had made her…how she longed to be full of him, stretched by him, pleasured endlessly only by him.

'There's nothing to be ashamed of if you are,' he pointed out softly. 'At one time it was quite usual for women to save themselves for their husbands—'

'Don't tease me,' she warned huskily.

'I'm not teasing you,' Alessandro assured her, kissing the

top of her head while his hands moved over her with long, calming strokes.

'I'm not very experienced,' Emily admitted, wanting more as she moved sinuously against him. 'And I'm twenty-eight,' she breathed provocatively, as if the time had come for him to remedy the situation.

'As old as that?' he growled, attending to her breasts.

Emily let out a soft cry as he began to suckle greedily whilst rolling the other nipple between a firm thumb and forefinger. He knew exactly how to tantalise her to the point of reason and beyond, until her body, her mind, her whole being craved only one thing.

'So what if you're not experienced?' Alessandro demanded, stopping to gaze at her. 'I think I know what you need…'

'Alessandro—'

'"Alessandro,"' he mocked softly, positioning her beneath him. She felt his breath fan her neck, and sighed as the shivers raced and competed with every other sensation delighting her senses.

'What's wrong, Emily?' he demanded, easing her thighs apart. 'Is it time to stop teasing you?'

'Alessandro,' Emily whispered putting her finger over his lips, 'don't hurt me…'

'I would never hurt you—'

'I don't mean that…I mean don't do this unless—'

'Unless?' He drew her hand to his lips to drop kisses on her soft palm. 'Tell me, Emily,' he insisted softly.

'I know this is just a marriage of convenience—'

He leaned back a little and stared at her thoughtfully. 'Is that all it is for you, Emily?'

'What is it for you?' she persisted, still craving reassurance.

'Our marriage is anything we choose to make of it,' Alessandro said, kissing each fingertip in turn. 'And in answer to your question, I would never hurt you…not intentionally.'

A starburst of emotion clouded her thoughts as he kissed her lips. His hands were growing more demanding, so she couldn't marshal her thoughts except to know that Alessandro was so skilled a lover… And she was lost.

Tugging off her skirt, he tossed it away and then returned his attention to her nipples. He began teasing them again with light passes of his fingertips, watching with satisfaction as she moaned and writhed beneath him.

Holding him captive with her fingers meshed through his hair, Emily savoured the touch of his mouth and his tongue, the nip of his teeth on her own swollen lips as his hands moved over her body transporting her to a fierce, elemental place where thought was nothing more than the slave of sensation. And now when he held back she played him at his own game, rolling away, luring him on.

But Alessandro was too fast and caught her easily, bringing her back beneath him and holding her firm between powerful thighs that seemed banded with steel. And now all that lay between them was a tiny white lace thong.

He had brought her to a highly aroused state, and Emily knew that it pleased him to see her so eager for his possession. Coaxing her thighs apart, he encouraged her to lift them for him, his amber eyes glittering with satisfaction as he used one hand to secure her arms above her head and the other to trace with a tantalisingly light touch the damp contours of the swell between her legs. She felt as if her whole being was concentrated in that one small area, as if every sensation she had ever experienced was magnified and centred there. Long, shuddering sighs told him how good it was, that it was the most intense sensation she had ever experienced, while Alessandro's murmurs to her in his own foreign tongue encouraged and enticed her all the more as he trailed his fingertips across the pouting site of her arousal.

When he tugged the thong off and she lay naked beneath him, wanting him so badly, there was a part of Emily that still held back at the thought of what such a powerful man might do to her. But even now Alessandro could sense her fear, and his hands were skilful and persuasive, making her forget everything but her desire for him. And when he dipped his fingertips between her wet swollen lips, the last of her doubts was erased by an intensity of sensation she could never have imagined. Crying out shamelessly, she begged him to take her then, but he refused to be hurried, only tempted her with the tip of his erection, pulling back just before she had a chance to draw him inside her. And then, releasing her hands, he gave her absolute freedom to decide the pace.

But once he was inside her Alessandro reclaimed control, increasing the pressure to fill her completely, stretching her beyond anything she could ever have imagined, until pleasure blanked out every thought but her craving for fulfillment. Holding her firm, he murmured reassurances, repeating her name when her sobbing cries marked the onset of the powerful spasms he had set up with such care.

Could anything ravish his senses more than this? Alessandro wondered, as he savoured the sight of Emily bucking beneath him.

Only one thing, perhaps, he realised as he plundered the moist, hidden depths of her mouth to taste her sweetness— and that would be the sight of his beautiful wife holding their child at the moment of its birth.

'I don't know if I like them,' Emily protested as Alessandro held out a linen cloth sagging with the weight of warm green figs plucked straight from the tree.

He made a sound of encouragement as he gave his collection a little shake. 'But ripe figs don't travel well,' he insisted. 'I promise you, Emily, you have never tasted anything like this before.'

128 THE PRINCE'S ARRANGED BRIDE

It was so hard to resist him… No, impossible, Emily realised as she gazed up into golden eyes whose beloved intensity had become so familiar to her over the past few days at Monte Volere. Did they only burn with fire like that when he looked at her? she wondered, smiling up at him as she picked out one of the plump ripe fruits and raised it to her lips. Even that innocent gesture seemed redolent with meaning now. She heard herself sigh, felt her body quiver with awareness…anticipation. She seemed to be in a permanent state of arousal…

After taking her to his bed in the homely old manor house Alessandro had introduced her to physical love in a way that made her want him all the time…every moment of every day, waking and even sleeping…so that she reached for him unknowing in the middle of the night, and then woke to find him making love to her again.

'Well?' he demanded softly as she sank her teeth into it.

Savouring the mouthful of intense, perfumed sweetness, Emily made a sound of contentment deep in her throat. 'It's the second best thing I ever put in my mouth,' she admitted, flashing him a glance.

Alessandro threw his head back and gave a short, virile laugh. 'Wait until you taste the wine from my vineyards,' he murmured provocatively. 'There are several contenders that should be considered before you make your mind up.'

'I won't change my mind,' Emily promised, slanting him a look as she linked her arm through his, relishing his strength and his body warmth through their light, summer-weight clothes.

'Ah, but my wine contains the essence of life,' Alessandro declared, laughing at her puzzled expression. 'You'll see what I mean when you drink it.'

He wasn't joking, Emily realised later, as she watched him select a bottle from the rack. She was even more surprised to see him moving about the well-equipped kitchen with a familiarity that suggested he was accustomed to fending for himself.

'Who taught you all this?' she demanded softly, linking her arms loosely around his waist as he whipped up an omelette. Leaning her face against his strong, muscular back, she inhaled his warm musky male scent… Being with him like this felt so wonderful…so right.

'Maria Felsina,' he said, reaching for the olive oil. 'Before she became a most sought-after dressmaker, specialising in traditional clothes, she lived with our family. She was the one who greeted me when I returned home from school for the holidays—from university, too. We spent more time together here at Monte Volere than at the palace. This is the one place where I can relax and be myself.'

'I can see that,' Emily agreed. 'Even at the grape-treading I noticed the way the people accepted you as one of them.'

'I am one of them,' Alessandro said simply. 'We all call Ferara home.'

'Did you see much of your parents when you were a child?'

'My parents were swept up in their duties at Court—'

'I hope you will find time for your own children—' Emily stopped, aghast, wondering how such words could shoot out of her mouth having made no connection first with her brain. She had no plans to have children, and was quite sure that Alessandro felt the same. Her cheeks were still on fire when he turned to look at her, and there was an expression on his face that seemed to confirm it would have been better to keep her opinions to herself. 'That is, when you have children eventually yourself—some time in the future,' she said, stumbling over the words.

The look of bewilderment, of sheer panic, on his wife's face pierced Alessandro's heart. 'Don't look at me like that, Emily,' he insisted, sweeping her into his arms. 'You've said nothing wrong.' Dipping his head, he stared deep into her eyes to assure her, 'I plan to have lots of children with the woman I love—and sooner rather than later.'

Alessandro forced back the urge to tell Emily about the final requirement before his father could retire. His desire had never been stronger, he realised as he pressed her to him. But now was not the time. Their love was little more than a tender shoot, and she was at her most vulnerable. He didn't know how she would react when he told her, and crucial business meetings were about to take him away. When he told her, he wanted the time to be right… He had to be there, to reassure her…

'Alessandro?' Pressing him away from her, Emily stood back. Did his silence mean some woman had been found for him…some woman who would bear his children…a fitting partner to rule Ferara alongside him?

'I wish I didn't have to go away,' he said tensely. 'But as you will discover, Emily, with great privilege comes great responsibility. You know I wouldn't think of leaving you unless there was absolutely no alternative.'

Did she? Emily wondered, staring up at him. But then he dragged her back into his arms, as if he couldn't bear to watch the doubts scudding across her face.

'Stop this, Emily!' he told her fiercely. 'When I am a father I will be with my children; I will take equal part in their up-bringing and I will spend as much time with them as any father, possibly more.'

'I believe you—'

'That's better,' he said, tipping the creamy egg mix into the pan. 'I cannot bear to see you upset. You'll feel better when you eat.'

If only it was that easy, Emily thought as she poured out two glasses of wine while Alessandro slid a delicious looking golden omelette onto a plate and dressed it with salad for her.

'You must promise me that you will stop worrying,' he insisted, nodding towards the table. 'I don't want to come home to a waif who has pined away. Haven't I told you, *cara mia*? Everything's going to be all right. My wife will take an equal part in everything I do.' He stopped in the act of pouring his own egg mix into the pan. 'What's wrong, Emily?'

Fork suspended, Emily could only stare at him. The idea of some other, unknown woman sitting so close to Alessandro, living with him…bearing his children…was insupportable.

'I promise you,' Alessandro said steadily, bringing his own food across to the table, 'we will share everything, and that's a promise.'

'Good,' Emily said, swallowing a huge mouthful of food, effectively staunching her end of the conversation. She tried not to choke on it as she considered the possibility that negotiations between Ferara and Alessandro's bride-to-be might be going on right at this very moment—even as they ate.

When was she ever going to accept that as soon as their contract came to an end Alessandro would want a proper marriage?

No time soon, she realised as they chinked glasses. But it was too late for regrets. She couldn't turn the clock back, and the truth was she was in love with her husband—deeply, passionately and ultimately, though she wished desperately it could be otherwise, hopelessly.

CHAPTER NINE

IT SEEMED no time at all since they had driven beneath the stone archway that marked the entrance to the Monte Volere estates to share their magical time, and now they were back in the Feraran capital, faced with reality. Even though Alessandro had reassured her about their impending separation, Emily felt as if her worst fears were taking on a darker, clearer shape. Alessandro had assured her that their parting would be for a couple of weeks at most. So why did she feel so sure it would be longer…?

This morning he would leave. The time for his departure had come around before she'd even had time to complete her move into his apartment at the palace, let alone discuss the worries that were now occupying her mind every waking moment. The little she had managed to glean about his trip left her in no doubt that it would be arduous, maybe even dangerous, and the last thing she wanted was to burden him with personal concerns…

Dressed casually for what she knew would be a rushed farewell, she waited in her old apartment, surrounded by all the chaos associated with her move. Pottering about aimlessly, she tried to concentrate on practical matters, picking up one thing, and then another, and switching their positions haphazardly in between glancing at her wristwatch as she counted down the minutes to his departure and wondered how much time they would have left together. Alessandro was already overrunning his schedule, and at the palace his daily life ran to a remorseless timetable.

'Emily, I'm so sorry.'

She nearly jumped out of her skin when he breezed into the room, but he came straight over to her and, seizing both of her hands in his, raised them to his lips.

'Forgive me, *cara sposa*—'

'Matters of State?' Emily teased softly, forcing a smile through the foretaste of loneliness that was already stealing into her mind. The last thing she wanted was to worry Alessandro in the last few moments they had together. She needed to know that he was oblivious to the undercurrents chipping away at her happiness, and felt a rush of relief when he grinned back at her.

'How I hate these distractions,' he murmured, tugging her towards him.

'What? Me?' Emily demanded fondly, staring into his eyes.

'Everything but you,' he growled softly. Pulling her over to the sofa, he insisted she sit down.

'You'll be late,' Emily reminded him, glancing at the delicate ormolu clock on her mantelpiece.

'So I'll be late for once. It's not something I make a habit of.' He paused and looked down at her, his dark golden gaze direct and full of warmth. 'But this is special.'

'What is?' Emily said curiously.

'You,' he said wryly, brushing a strand of hair away from her face. 'For you I would make the whole world stand in line and wait, because I love you. I love you more than life itself, Emily. Forgive me for leaving you, but know that, however much you miss me, I shall miss you more.'

Tentatively Emily traced the line of Alessandro's claret-coloured silk tie from the point where it secured the crisp white collar around her husband's strong, tanned neck, down his toned torso to the slim black leather belt on his midnight-blue suit.

'And I love you more than I ever thought it possible to love anyone,' she whispered. 'I have never trusted anyone so completely in my life—with my life—you are my life.'

Bringing her hands to his lips, Alessandro turned them and kissed each palm in turn. 'For ever, Emily,' he murmured, looking deep into her eyes. 'And now…' The corners of his mouth were starting to tug up in a grin. 'I've got something for you.'

Shifting emotional gears in tandem, Emily threw him an amused look. 'A crown?' she teased, remembering the last occasion on which he had said something similar.

'Not a crown,' he said with a wry shrug. 'I could get one for you, but I thought you weren't so keen on that type of thing.'

She loved the way his eyes crinkled at the corners when he grinned at her like that. 'OK, so don't keep me in suspense.'

Reaching inside his jacket, Alessandro drew out a slim volume of poetry. 'Christopher Marlowe,' he murmured softly as he pressed it into her hands. 'Well, Emily, do you like it? Does it please you?'

'It pleases me very much,' Emily whispered as she traced the worn binding reverently with her fingertips. He couldn't have brought her anything she would have liked more, she realised. 'I love it,' she whispered. 'It's the most beautiful…the most special thing I've ever been given.'

'I was hoping you would say that,' he said, cupping her chin to draw her forward for a tender kiss on the lips. 'Because I want you to read a page every day while I am away, and then you will know how much I love you. And now—'

'You must leave?' Emily said, trying to be brave about it.

'Soon,' he agreed, putting his finger over her lips.

She pulled away. 'I'm sorry, Alessandro. I feel so—'

'How?' he demanded softly. 'Emily, speak to me.'

'Once the terms of our contract are satisfied—' She shook her head, unable to go on.

'You can't stop there,' he warned.

'Has a bride been found for you?' She spoke so softly she couldn't be sure at first that he had heard.

'A bride *has* been found,' Alessandro confirmed. 'But I found her myself, and she is sitting here in front of me now.'

'So, you really do love me?'

Alessandro's brows rose as he stared at her, and when he spoke again his voice had adopted the low, teasing tone she loved so much. 'You guessed,' he teased gently with a heavy sigh. 'I guess that means my secret's out.'

As he brought her into his arms Emily felt safe again, as if her fears had been of her own conjuring—and all for nothing.

'I love you,' she murmured against his lips. 'But I don't know how I am going to live without you.'

He put his finger over her lips and smiled into her eyes before replacing his finger with his lips. 'You don't have to live without me, *mio tesoro*,' he said at last. 'This will just be a very brief separation.'

'Promise?'

'I promise,' he vowed softly, wrapping her fingers around the book of poems as he got to his feet. But at the door he stopped, and dragged her to him. 'I'd take you with me, but—'

'I'll be fine. Go,' she whispered fiercely, 'before you change your mind.'

'I have already changed my mind,' Alessandro confessed, raking his fingers impatiently through his hair.

'But you're running late,' Emily murmured without much conviction as he dragged her back into his arms.

'One of the privileges of being a prince is that I set the

agenda,' he husked against her ear. 'And I have just remembered something very important…something that cannot wait…'

'Here?' Emily breathed, feeling her heart pound against his chest as he pressed her back against the door.

Miming that she should be quiet for a moment, Alessandro dug in his pocket for his mobile phone. 'File a new flight plan,' he ordered briefly when the call was connected. 'I have been unavoidably delayed.'

In the short time since Alessandro had been away, Emily had to admit that one of her greatest successes had been his father's apartment. With his approval she had transformed it, relegating the angular, uncomfortable furniture to the areas of the palace she thought might eventually be opened to the public and replacing it with a selection of well-padded armchairs, cosy throws and rugs. A small kitchen had been created, and a supply of fresh fruit, cakes and other delicacies were ordered to be delivered on a daily basis.

'You've done too much for me already,' he protested one day, while Emily was balanced on the top of a pair of stepladders, fixing some dried autumnal arrangements to the wall.

Turning quickly to reply, she paused and put a hand to her forehead. She never usually felt dizzy…

'Why don't we call one of the servants to do that for you?' he suggested.

Hearing the anxiety in his voice, Emily hurried to reassure him, realising he had been on his feet helping her for most of the morning. 'I'm fine,' she said. 'Are you getting tired?'

'No, it's you I'm thinking about,' he said. 'Why don't you come down from there? You look pale.'

'Don't worry about…' As her voice faded Emily blinked her eyes several times, fighting for equilibrium. She had never fainted in her life before, or been sick, but all at once it felt as if she was going to do both.

'I'm sorry, I think I'm going to be—' Hand over mouth,

she slid cartoon-style down the stepladder, and made a dash for the bathroom.

She got there just in time. Turning on the cold tap, she filled the basin and immersed her face in the icy water. Then, pulling back, she looked at herself in the mirror. Wet-faced and ashen, she steadied herself against the wall. She was no fool, she knew all the signs: she was pregnant. The only problem now was how was she ever going to bear the wait until Alessandro returned.

'Are you all right in there?'

'Yes, I'm fine,' she called brightly. Hurriedly wiping her face on a towel and arranging her hair as best she could in just a few seconds, she swung open the door, making sure she had a reassuring smile on her face for Alessandro's father. 'Let's get back to those catkins and hazel twigs,' she said as she walked past him.

'No, no,' young lady,' he said, waggling his finger at her. 'You've done more than enough for one day in your condition—'

'My condition?'

He couldn't conceal the sparkle in his eyes as he looked at her. 'You know what I mean,' he insisted, ushering her to a chair. 'I'm only surprised my son hasn't thought to inform me.'

'Inform you? What should Alessandro have told you?'

The old Prince considered this in silence for a few moments, then his face crumpled with concern. 'You mean he doesn't know yet?'

'That I'm pregnant? Emily said with a shy smile. 'No, Alessandro doesn't know about our baby yet. I've only just found out myself. But I'll tell him the moment he returns—'

'He should have been the first.'

'These things happen,' Emily said with a shrug as she smiled back at him.

'He'll return soon—immediately,' Alessandro's father

amended thoughtfully. 'I'll have a messenger dispatched to bring him back here at once.'

'Could you do that?' Emily said, hardly daring to believe that Alessandro might be back with her so soon.

'Of course. And as soon as Alessandro knows about the baby we can make the announcement.'

'Won't it be a little early to go public with the news of my pregnancy?' Emily said with concern.

'Excuse my eagerness, but as well as celebrating my first grandchild I shall be celebrating my freedom.'

'Your freedom? What do you mean?'

'I shall be free…free to concentrate on my roses,' he explained excitedly. Now that you are expecting the heir I can abdicate formally. Forgive me, Emily. I am so eager to renounce the throne and pass it on to Alessandro I can hardly think straight.'

'What did you mean about making the announcement of my pregnancy official…before you can abdicate?' Emily said carefully.

'Alessandro must have explained—'

'Of course,' she said quickly. 'But it's always good to hear it again. I have so much yet to learn about my new country.' She felt as if each separate word was being wrenched out of her, and each one of them caused her pain—pain that only increased when she saw the expression of suppressed excitement, of longing, and of a dream so close now he could almost touch it written clear across her father-in-law's face.

'Well, as you know,' he began, struggling to keep his excitement under control, 'the first condition was that my son should marry before I could contemplate abdication—'

'Contemplate…' Emily murmured.

'That's right. Marriage, of course, was the first step. And the announcement of your pregnancy…the birth of your child, Alessandro's heir…is what my country's archaic legislation requires before I can abdicate in his favour. I never mentioned it before…for reasons of delicacy,' he explained gently. 'I know you can't force these things—'

Oh, can't you? Emily thought, feeling as if her heart had just splintered into a thousand little pieces. 'No,' she agreed huskily. 'That's true.'

'But now, with this wonderful news…wonderful for all of us,' he said expansively, opening his arms in an embrace-the-world gesture. 'Emily, come to me. Let me thank you for this gift of life.'

Like an automaton, Emily accepted the old Prince's arms around her shoulders and even managed to return his kiss. He had done nothing wrong, she reasoned. She couldn't blame Alessandro's father for his son's *oversight*…

Oversight, Emily thought incredulously, much later alone in her own room. She hadn't even moved fully into Alessandro's apartment at the palace and now she was pregnant with his child. Everything that seemed to have been built on firm foundations between them had been founded on a lie. There was only one thing left to do now—and it didn't involve staying a minute longer than she had to in Ferara.

Picking up the telephone, she called her sister's mobile.

'What do you mean, she's gone?'

His father looked at him in anguish. 'I said she should tell you—'

'Tell me what?' Alessandro demanded in a clipped voice devoid of emotion. 'I'm sorry, Father,' he said, shaking his head as if he had never been more disappointed with himself. 'None of this is your fault. If I hadn't been visiting such a volatile place I would have taken Emily with me and none of this would have happened.'

'I think it's more complicated than that,' the elderly Prince ventured cautiously.

'What do you mean?'

Clapping his son on the shoulder, the old man let his hand

linger for a squeeze of paternal affection. 'I'm sorry, Alessandro. I can't tell you—'

'Can't tell me!' Alessandro exploded. 'What can't you tell me about my wife? Has she been unfaithful to me?'

'No!' the old Prince exclaimed with outrage. 'She has not.'

'Then what?' Alessandro demanded angrily. 'Why else would she leave me?'

'You left her…*here…alone*,' his father reminded him. 'A stranger in our country, young and vulnerable. She was lonely—'

'We had an arrangement,' Alessandro reminded him bitterly.

'An arrangement?' his father exclaimed incredulously. 'If that's all you think of your marriage, Alessandro, then perhaps Emily was right to go.'

'Right! She is my wife!' Alessandro thundered. 'And whether you like it or not, Father, we have an arrangement—'

'Bah! Don't talk to me of arrangements, Alessandro,' he warned. 'I'll have none of it. I will not have my happiness at Emily's expense…or yours,' he added, seeing the torment that was fast replacing the anger on his son's face.

Mashing his lips together in impotent fury, Alessandro turned his back and stalked to the window. 'Then where is she?' he growled in an undertone.

'Somewhere where she is appreciated, I imagine,' his father told him mildly.

'And where might that be?' Alessandro said, turning slowly on his heels to confront him again.

'I'll leave you to work that out. But don't take too long, Alessandro. Don't let her slip through your fingers.'

Grinding his jaws together, Alessandro sucked in a breath as he made his decision. 'If she really wants to go, Father, there is nothing I can do to stop her. But if there is even the slightest chance—'

'You're wasting precious time, Alessandro.'

Inclining his head in a curt show of silent agreement, Alessandro paused only to give his father a brief, fierce embrace before setting off for his own rooms, where he would pack an overnight bag and ring the airport to file his flight plan for London.

'As it happens, Emily, I do have something for you. Something I think you'll like—the fallout from a nice juicy bankruptcy. Your clients are major creditors—after the usual banks and Inland Revenue et cetra. Respectable elderly couple, allegedly fleeced out of their life savings by some toff from the Shires.'

'Billy, you're a diamond,' Emily said gratefully, playing to her Chief Clerk, whose thick Cockney accent and market stall *joie de vivre* masked a mind of Brobdingagian scope and efficiency. She had been expecting to pick up the dregs on her return to Chambers—the cases no one else wanted. But this was right up her street. 'Do we have all the papers?'

'Do pigs have wings? But your clients are available for a conference this morning.'

'Good. Give me what we've got. Set up the meeting. Oh, and Billy?'

'Yes?'

'If any personal calls come through for me…I'm not available.'

'I understand,' Billy said non-committally, straightening his impeccable tailor-made waistcoat on his rapid passage out of the room.

Collecting up her things, Emily went to settle herself into the office Billy had allocated to her. She was back to being a 'door tenant' for the time being—a part-timer in Chambers—and would have to submit to being shuffled about wherever there was available space.

Across Europe the new generation of young royals all

combined professional careers with the responsibilities of their rank, so there hadn't been a single comment when she'd returned to work. And by using her maiden name she was largely assured of anonymity. So far, at least, the paparazzi had failed to mark any change in the blissful state of the Crown Prince of Ferara's marriage.

It had been Miranda's suggestion that she return to work and take time to think things through. They stuck by each other through thick and thin, Emily mused, knowing she needed her sister's support like never before. She knew Miranda would never suggest she should try and forget there had ever been a man called Alessandro…but that wasn't going to stop her trying, Emily thought as she reached for the intercom button.

'Billy, can you bring those papers in right away, please?'

The meeting with her elderly clients went well. As Emily had anticipated, they were both dressed in their Sunday best, and trying their hardest to appear at ease, when in fact, after planning carefully all their lives to enjoy a well-earned retirement, they were now staring into the abyss. Fortunately they had kept a meticulous diary of events, and with that she could build a case.

Emily found nothing unusual in taking over a case at the last minute, but it did mean that crucial parts of the thick file had to be read and assimilated before the first court hearing that same afternoon. Fortunately she thrived on the pressure; cases like these were what had attracted her to law in the first place.

She broke concentration reluctantly when a knock came at the door, knowing it could only be one person.

'Sorry to disturb you, Emily,' said Billy. 'I thought you should know you've had one call.'

'From?'

'Your sister.'

'Oh?' Emily said with concern.

'She said not to worry you.'

But the way Billy had delivered the message suggested she should look deeper into the matter without delay, Emily thought, automatically scanning her diary. 'Could you get hold of her for me, please, Billy?'

'Already on line one,' he announced briskly, on his way out of the door.

'Miranda?'

'Sorry to trouble you at work, Em. I know you left a message with Billy to say you were too busy to speak to anyone, but I thought you should know—'

'You don't have to apologise.'

'Alessandro's in town. He wants to see you. I didn't know what to say.'

Emily's heart must have stopped. She only knew she had never been more grateful for her sister's support at the other end of the line. 'Did you tell him?'

'Where you'll be? No. I'm waiting for you to give me the go-ahead on that. But, Emily?' Miranda added anxiously.

'Yes?'

'I really think you should see him. At least give him a chance to explain.'

'I don't know.'

'Please, Em. If you'd spoken to him, heard how worried he sounds, you wouldn't be so hard on him. He knows you're appearing in court today; he just doesn't know which one…'

The silence hung between them and deepened, until finally Emily said softly, 'I can't keep running away from him for ever, can I, Miranda?'

Dragging the documents she had been reading before the call back towards her, Emily read the name of the man she would be accusing in court that day—the man who had tricked and betrayed an elderly couple. Alessandro had betrayed and tricked *her*, she remembered bitterly—and into a marriage of convenience that included an innocent child. What sort of man did that?

Alessandro managed to slip into the visitors' gallery just as the court usher called out, 'All rise,' and the judge walked in and took her seat.

He missed the first few moments of procedure—case number, names, et cetera—and was barely aware that another man, seeing him arrive, had also moved into the gallery a couple of rows back, and was desperately trying to catch his attention. The only thing he saw, the only thing he cared about, was Emily, fully robed and bewigged, standing in front of the judge.

He drank her in like a life-restoring draught, feeling his resolve and his determination increase with every second that he gazed at her. Just being so close was like a healing process, and he hadn't even realised how heartsick he was until this moment. He was in such agony he had to clench his fists to stop himself calling out to her. Taking a deep breath, he battled to compose himself. He would win her back. He had to…

His heart sang with pride while his mind seethed with questions as reason and logic made a steady return. Staring at her, he found it impossible to equate the woman he'd thought he knew—the clear-faced, intelligent woman below him now in the well of the court—with someone who could give herself to a man as freely and as lovingly as Emily had and then simply disappear without a word. Had she fallen out of love with him? His guts churned as an ugly worm of suspicion burrowed into his mind.

He had been so sure that she loved him—but then how could she have left him so abruptly if that was so? And, feelings apart, she had broken the contract that meant so much to her—to her sister. His father was heartbroken by their split, yet Emily had said she loved him, too. What could have taken her from them without even the basic courtesy of a note…something…anything to explain her behaviour? It had to be something so momentous, he reasoned, that only a face-to-face meeting would allow it to be brought out into the open. Yet a face-to-face meeting was the very thing Emily seemed intent on avoiding—but she *would* meet with him, he was determined on that…

The efforts of the man sitting behind Alessandro to attract his attention failed until the judge called a mid-morning recess. The very last thing on Alessandro's mind was a reunion with someone from his old school. Let alone Archibald Freemantle, he realised, grinding his jaw as he fought to remain civil.

His whole mind was focused on one thing and one thing only, and that was making things right with his wife. Maybe his pride had taken a battering when she deserted him, but the overriding emotion he had felt then, as now, was one of loss. Loss so insupportable he had no strategy to cope with the devastating effect it was having on every aspect of his life. Without Emily he had no life, Alessandro thought bitterly, forcing his attention back to the irritating individual in front of him.

'Archibald,' he said coolly, extending his hand as courtesy demanded, then removing it as fast as good manners allowed. 'What brings you here?'

'This case, old boy,' Archibald exclaimed, with such a heartfelt sigh it threatened to mist up his gold-rimmed spectacles.

'Oh?' Alessandro said vaguely, trying to be discreet about his desire to spot Emily…if only for a moment…just a glance would do, he realised, cursing himself for being a lovesick fool.

'You must have realised it's m'brother,' Archibald said, huffing again. 'Freemantle Minor,' he clarified, reverting to the argot of school.

Alessandro tensed. It didn't seem quite the moment to

comment, *Oh, that rat,* so he confined himself to a murmured, 'Ah, now I recognise him.' The man in the dock, he realised, and a flash of amusement briefly eased his torment. Toby Freemantle had started his career as a small-time crook, going through coat pockets at school—until he was asked to leave. It appeared he had pursued his calling into adult life.

'Would have got off,' Archibald said hotly, clearly determined to elicit Alessandro's support, 'had it not been for that bitch barrister the wrinklies hired. Apparently she's hot stuff—said to be one of the best legal minds around. For a woman,' he added scornfully.

Rage powered up through Alessandro's frame at this casual dismissal of Emily's abilities, but only a muscle flexing in his jaw threatened to betray his feelings.

'I'm sure the judge presiding would be delighted to hear you make such a remark,' he commented laconically. 'Oh, and by the way, Archibald…'

'Yes?'

'That woman is my wife.'

Making a hasty exit, Emily was keen to escape to Chambers, where she could forget her personal problems and immerse herself in the case ready for cross-examination the next day.

Head down, arms encircling her bundle of papers, secured with the traditional pink ties, she failed to see the tall, imposing figure waiting at the head of the broad sweep of marble steps… Until an arm reached in front of her to grab hold of the mahogany banister and block her way.

'Emily—can we talk?'

Her mind locked with shock, even though she had expected Alessandro to find her. Unable to cope with the thought of seeing him again, she had simply banished it from her mind.

Seeing the security guards on alert, and moving towards them fast, Emily nodded them away first before she spoke. 'Alessandro. I didn't expect to see you here.'

Why was she lying to him? She bit down on her lip. All her cool, all her reserve, every bit of the calm logic that guided her in the courtroom had vanished.

It was useless reminding herself that this was the man who had lied to her, who had used her like a breeding mare to gain an heir for his country, when the need to feel his arms around her instead of having one of them obstruct her path in such a stiff and telling way was all she cared about.

She could hardly breathe. She couldn't bring herself to look at him. But then, she didn't need to, she realised wretchedly. She could feel him, sense him, scent his clean male warmth and imbibe his very essence without using her eyes.

If she didn't keep his betrayal, his lie of omission at the forefront of her mind, she might just go mad from wanting him.

'Emily, please…won't you even speak to me?'

She wouldn't survive if he hurt her again. 'This is a difficult case—'

'I can see that. I'm sorry to intrude on your work, but your phone is always switched through to your answering service.'

'I don't have much time—'

'As I said, I apologise for approaching you like this, but I could think of no other way.'

The whole situation was a catastrophic mess, Emily realised tensely. Leaving aside her own feelings, Miranda's first solo concert was coming up in the New Year—a concert where she would be playing the violin Alessandro had loaned to her.

'Emily—' Alessandro's voice had roughened, and was considerably louder. It brought her back to full attention. 'I have to talk to you,' he insisted. 'But not here; not like this, please.'

Emily's face flushed red as she stared up at him. She had never thought to hear so needy, so desperate a note in his voice.

'I know I've let you down—'

He had found out she knew about the baby clause; she

could hear it in his voice…in what he didn't say. She had to hear his explanation. 'I feel as if I hardly know you any more,' she murmured, speaking her thoughts out loud.

'Well, I only know that I've hurt you, Emily. And that I can't let it end like this. I can't go on any more without your forgiveness.'

My forgiveness…my forgiveness, Emily thought wretchedly as her hand moved instinctively to cover her stomach. 'If you could give me the rest of the afternoon…'

'You have to eat,' he said instantly. 'Why don't we meet at my hotel for dinner? Eight o'clock? You won't want a late night.'

'Yes… Yes, please.'

'Shall I send a car for you?'

Her mind was in freefall. She needed time to think, to prepare, to plan how she was going to tell him about their baby. 'No, that's fine. I'd rather you didn't.'

Emily stood motionless, watching Alessandro take the steps down to the foyer. He moved with long, purposeful strides, his head held high, and the gaze of every woman, and not a few of the men, zoned in on his rapid departure.

Only when he had gone through the doors that led to the street did she begin very slowly to follow after him. He was still her husband…and in spite of everything she knew without doubt she still loved him.

She fought hard in court…wasn't her marriage worth fighting for, too?

The invisible men, as Emily had learned to call them, had obviously telephoned ahead, as the door to Alessandro's suite swung open before she could even knock.

As he stood back to let her pass the temptation to touch him, to look into his eyes, was almost irresistible. But she could feel remoteness coming off him in waves, pushing her away.

Shrugging off her winter coat and scarf, she put them on

a chair first, and then, having first drawn a deep, steadying breath, she turned around. 'How are you, Alessandro?'

He looked amazing. Black trousers, black round-necked cashmere sweater framing his tan...

'How am I?' he said, dipping his head to give her a keen look. 'That's an interesting question, coming from you, Emily.'

Picking up her coat and scarf, he walked across the room and deposited them inside what must be a cloakroom.

'Apparently I'm some sort of monster,' he said with his back to her, 'since my wife walked out on me without a word of explanation.'

CHAPTER TEN

THE expression in her husband's eyes frightened Emily. It was as if all the angry frustration, all the bafflement possible had been captured and condensed in his gaze. And as for herself... She took a steadying breath and struggled to find the words she had so carefully rehearsed in the taxi from her apartment. But she was in too much pain to speak—pain so bad it felt as if her heart had been ripped out of her chest and stamped on.

It seemed like several lifetimes before she managed to say, 'I spoke to your father—'

'And?'

She had never heard him sounding so curt, so cold. And she wasn't doing much better. Her own voice was strangulated, false. She had to wait and take a few deep breaths before she could relax enough to start again. 'He told me—'

'Told you what?' Alessandro cut in harshly. Why was it that angry words hung in the air longer than any others? he wondered furiously. The very last thing he had intended to do was shout at Emily the moment she arrived, but his emotions were in turmoil. No one knew better than he that the rest of their lives depended on what happened between them in the next few hours. 'Go on,' he said, making a conscious effort to soften his tone.

Emily knew she had to set him straight about his father's

role, if nothing else. 'It was something he thought I already knew…something he believed you would have told me,' she went on, trying to stay calm. 'He said he couldn't abdicate until you…until I had your child.'

Alessandro's face went blank and unreadable—like a stranger's, Emily realised with an inward shudder. She saw the change come into his eyes first: a slow infusion of pain, then guilt, and finally something approaching fear.

'I thought I'd lose you,' he said, so softly she could hardly make out the words. 'I believed it was too much for you to accept all at once. You would never have agreed—'

'You're right about that,' Emily flared, her own voice shaking with emotion. 'I would never have agreed to barter the life of a child—even for the sake of my own sister's happiness.' She stopped. There was an iron band around her chest; she could hardly breathe. She wheeled away from him in bewilderment. 'I thought you loved me,' she cried accusingly.

In a couple of strides Alessandro had crossed the room and grabbed her chin, forcing her to look up at him.

'Don't you understand anything, Emily? I do love you. More than you will ever know. No! Look at me!' he insisted when she tried to turn her head away. 'I love you,' he repeated fiercely. 'I have loved you from the first moment I set eyes on you. I don't suppose you believe in love at first sight; neither did I, before I met you—' He shook his head and looked away, as if the emotion was too much for him to bear. 'I was frightened I might lose you if I told you the truth. I can see now that I was wrong. But if you won't accept my apology then I don't know what I can do…what I will do without you…'

'When would you have told me?' Emily demanded tensely when he'd let her go.

'If you had become pregnant there would have been no need to tell you,' he admitted with a short, humourless laugh.

'That's very blunt.'

'Yes,' he agreed bitterly.

'And if I hadn't become pregnant?' She needed to choose her words with more care, Emily realised distractedly, still agonising over her own startling news and wondering how she was going to break it to him. 'When…when would you have told me?'

'I'm not sure,' Alessandro admitted bluntly. 'I needed time…time to be sure you trusted me before I could identify the *right time*.'

'I see.'

'No, you don't,' he said, taking hold of her again. 'I was wrong. I can see that now. I should have told you right away. I need you to forgive me, Emily. I need you to accept my apology so that we can rebuild everything I have damaged, however long it takes… Emily?'

When she told him about their baby—what would he think of her then? Emily wondered numbly. He had been so honest, so frank and giving in his own apology, while she harboured the greatest secret of them all, jealously guarding it inside her like some precious gift she had not yet chosen to bestow. Instead of making it easier for her, Emily realised, Alessandro's openness had only made it all the more difficult.

'This isn't easy for you,' he said. 'I realise that. You need time to think. I'm going to take you home. No, I insist,' he said, holding up his hands. 'I'll keep in touch, and when you're ready—'

'No,' Emily said urgently—this wasn't supposed to happen. 'I don't want you to take me home.' This was the moment. She needed to tell him…whatever the consequences might be for herself.

She could see how pale he was beneath his tan, hear the enormous pressure he was forced to endure because of her reflected in his voice. She couldn't bear it. She couldn't bear to see him suffering and know that she was the cause.

'Don't apologise to me. We're both at fault,' she said, the

words all coming out in a rush. 'We had no chance to get to know each other—'

'Listen to yourself,' he said. 'You're half-frantic with worry, and all because of me. There's no excuse for my behaviour,' he said harshly, cutting off any chance she might have had to say more. 'I'm going to get your coat—'

'No, Alessandro, wait—'

But he was already back, and helping her into it. 'I'm taking you home, Emily. I've upset you enough for one night. I won't hear any arguments.'

But her home was in Ferara, Emily thought as he ushered her out of the door. With Alessandro...

'I don't want to pressure you,' he said, releasing his hold on her arm at the door to her apartment. 'I've put you through enough. If you come back to me, Emily, it will be for ever, so I want you to be sure.'

'We never expected it to come to this.' Emily shivered suddenly as he kissed her on both cheeks, as if in that moment the shadow between them had made itself visible.

'We never expected to fall in love,' Alessandro countered softly, shooting her a wry half-smile as he turned to go.

Emily had thought she'd had sleepless nights before, but she'd been wrong. *This*...this was a sleepless night.

Finally she gave up on sleep altogether, and, clambering out of bed, crossed the wood-strip floor to the enclosed balcony that had been one of her main reasons for buying the riverside flat.

She could never have anticipated that her meeting with Alessandro would go so badly wrong...that she would be so lacking in force, in ability to put her point across. She was ashamed of the way she had caved in, Emily realised tensely. But the atmosphere had been so fraught, their reunion so fragile... If Miranda had been at home they would have talked things over. But Miranda had already embarked on a

tour of the provinces that preceded her debut in the capital…
And, though she had lost track of time, Emily knew it was
the middle of the night—Miranda would be asleep.

Wrapping herself in a mohair throw, she curled up on
one of the sofas and stared bleakly out at the river, stretching darkly into the distance like an oily rag. The main road
was freshly salted with icy sleet and made her long all the
more for the mellow colours and warmth and sunshine of
Ferara.

Whatever time it was, her mind was still buzzing. She
hadn't managed to sleep since Alessandro had left a little after
twelve. Burrowing deeper into the soft throw, she squeezed
her eyes tightly shut and wished harder than she had ever
wished for anything in her life that things could be different…
Wasn't cheating a man out of his child on a par with cheating
a defenceless elderly couple out of their life savings?

The unmistakable sound of her laptop signalling incoming
mail broke into that disturbing thought, and, peering at the
clock, she saw that it still wasn't quite four-thirty in the
morning.

Racking her brains for friends in the Antipodes, or even
late-working New Yorkers, she padded across acres of wood-
strip flooring into the open-plan space that constituted her
living area. Leaning over her desk, she clicked the mouse and
brought up the screen.

*Tight schedule—now leaving first thing tomorrow—
make your decision about returning to Ferara—let me
know soonest—Alessandro.*

Her heart gave a little flurry just to know that he was
awake—and thinking of her. But, reading the e-mail again,
she went cold. She couldn't leave London. There was still the
court case to settle. And it wasn't going well; there were all
sorts of outstanding issues.

Fingers flying, she typed a reply and sent it straight back.

I can't make that sort of decision yet. I have a tight schedule, too.

She hovered anxiously over the machine, realising that he couldn't read her mind and know all the difficulties she was facing at work. Out of context the message would just seem petulant.

His reply came through right away.

I understand you need more time.

Frowning a little, Emily pulled out her chair and sat down in front of the computer.

The case I'm involved in is proving more complex than I had anticipated.

This time she gave herself a little more space before touching 'send', and checked what she had typed again for possible misunderstandings. She hugged herself as she waited for Alessandro's reply. It didn't take long.

When will your case be completed?
Difficult to say. Two weeks max, at a guess.
Before the holidays?
Hopefully before the holidays.
I'll send the jet.
No need.
But that's a yes?

She hesitated about ten heartbeats—a split second.

Yes.
I'll send the jet.

Emily sat staring at the screen until dawn sketched rosy fingers across a sullen, snow-laden sky, but there was no more mail that night from Alessandro.

Touching the screen by his name before she switched off, she wondered what lay ahead for them both with the holidays approaching fast. The possibility of seeing him again was the only present she had on her Christmas list.

Unforeseen delay in resolving case—no chance I can make it for Christmas.
Sorry.
Emily

Alessandro took out his frustration on his desk with a blow so hard he found himself nursing his fist, wondering if he had broken anything.

He had chosen e-mail specifically as a mode of communication to give them both a breather. A voice on a telephone could reveal so much…too much. E-mail was brief and to the point. And utterly without emotion—or should be…had always been…up to now.

Hating himself for putting his heart on the line, he stabbed back.

What's the problem?

Sitting in her office, surrounded by papers, Emily rested her forehead on the heel of her hand and stared at the screen. She felt sick from early pregnancy blues augmented by a very real concern for her clients. It was beginning to look as though she would win the case, but the chance of securing some money for the elderly couple was appearing increasingly unlikely.

The likelihood of reaching any type of satisfactory conclusion before the long drawn-out holiday season interrupted everything was negligible.

She touched the screen by Alessandro's question, as if it was possible to draw some comfort from him by doing that, then pulled her hand away. Having him at the other end of the line, waiting for her reply, was no compensation for having him with her. And knowing he was out there somewhere, but not knowing where, made her feel lonelier than ever. It made her feel weak and vulnerable—something she could have done without. Because that was no help to her elderly clients, whose future peace of mind lay in the scrambled mounds of documentation scattered across her desk. But the least she owed Alessandro was an explanation for staying in London over Christmas…

Freemantle has no money—no assets—no nothing. Can't leave my clients in the lurch—have to keep trying.

Try what? Emily thought, absentmindedly dispatching the message before she had quite finished it. If Toby Freemantle was stony broke—

Her eyes flashed to the screen as Alessandro's reply came up.

Trace his maternal grandmother's will. She left him all her art treasures. His brother boasted to me that whenever creditors came to call the paintings were stored in their mother's attic. Keep me informed. Alessandro.

Instantly alert, Emily straightened up, and tapped in. *Thank you—I will.*

And then, not because she thought it was prudent, or that

he would even care, but because her heart took over, she lapsed into a personal style.

I hope you have a good Christmas, Alessandro—say sorry from me to your father. Emily.

Making a sound close to a tiger in a rage, Alessandro replied.

Sure to—Father in South Africa, looking at rose gardens—signing off, Alessandro.

Alessandro had been right, Emily thought, waving off two very happy elderly people, her hands clutching tight the bottle of champagne they had insisted on buying for her. She wouldn't drink it now, because she was almost four months pregnant, but it signified their peace of mind, and that was all that mattered. She would take it to the Christmas gathering at her parents' house.

Thanks to Alessandro, the works of art she had tracked down with the help of the fraud squad had raised millions at auction, brightening the London scene on the run-up to the big Christmas shut-down. There had been more than enough money to satisfy all the creditors and even set Toby Freemantle up for life—when he came out of jail.

As the elderly couple disappeared around the corner, arm in arm, she knew her first e-mail had to be to Alessandro. She had to thank him, let him know the outcome of the sale.

Great news—do you ski?

Rocking back on her chair, Emily stared at the screen again.

Almost as hesitantly as she might have said the words, she tapped in, *Yes—why?* then clicked the mouse and waited.

We have issues to resolve sooner rather than later. I plan to spend Christmas in a small village called Lech, in the Arlberg region of Austria. I'd like you to join me.

Emily's heart leapt at the invitation. But she had promised to attend her mother's famous Christmas lunch, she remembered, frowning.

'Of course you must go with Alessandro,' Miranda insisted, when Emily telephoned her twin to run the idea past her. 'You don't think Mother will try and make you stay in England if she thinks there's a chance of a *rapprochement* with Alessandro, do you?'

'No, but—'

'But what?'

'I haven't told him yet,' Emily said tensely, tracing her still flat stomach.

'Are you going to wait until he can see for himself?'

'I don't know. I—'

'Look, Emily,' Miranda said, beginning to sound impatient. 'I've got to go to rehearsal. You're the one who always knows what to do. You know what you have to do now. You're just allowing emotion to get in the way of clear thinking.'

Emily allowed herself a wry smile. 'Are you surprised?'

'That you've let things go this far? Yes. It's a fact that Alessandro wasn't entirely open with you. Get over it. Aren't you doing just the same to him now? If you want the truth, it looks like a bad case of double standards.'

'Please don't be angry with me. You know I've forgiven him. But he wouldn't give me a chance to explain—'

Miranda heaved a heavy sigh down the phone, cutting her off. 'I'm not angry with you, Emily. I'm just worried about you—and Alessandro. Please say you'll go.'

'I can't just turn up pregnant in Lech.'

'No, you can't,' Miranda agreed thoughtfully. 'So maybe I'll—'

'No! Don't you dare say a word to him,' Emily warned. 'This is something I have to handle by myself.'

'Promise?'

'Have I ever let you down?'

'This would be one hell of a time to make it a first,' Miranda said bluntly.

Emily could feel her sister's concern winging down the phone-line. 'I won't let you down, Miranda. I promise.'

After doing her research, Emily knew why her husband had chosen Lech for his winter retreat—the townsfolk were so used to visiting royalty no one paid the slightest attention to one more prince arriving for the winter sports. She realised now that any type of anonymity was preferable to none.

It wouldn't take her long to pack a suitcase, book a flight—

She swung around in surprise when the doorbell rang. She wasn't expecting anyone and, apart from kicking off her high-heeled shoes, she hadn't even changed her clothes after the final meeting with her clients. Checking her appearance in the mirror, she pulled a face and made a vain attempt to capture some of her long hair into the slide at the back of her head. Reaching the door, she opened it and gasped.

'Alessandro! Wh—?'

'May I come in?'

'Yes, of course. But—' Her bewildered gaze followed him across the wide expanse of floor to the picture windows, where he turned and stood looking around him, the corners of his mouth pressing up in an appreciative grin.

'This is very nice,' he said, looking around the apartment.

'Thank you,' she said. Shutting the door, Emily leaned back against it. Her heart-rate had gone into orbit…she needed a minute. No, a minute wasn't nearly long enough, she realised, staring at her husband.

His charcoal-grey vicuña overcoat had been left open to reveal a black V-neck cashmere sweater and black trousers, and his inky-black hair in its customary off-duty disarray fell over familiar dark gold eyes—eyes that were presently trained on her with amused speculation.

'I don't understand—I was just e-mailing you—'

'And you presumed I was in Ferara?'

She could see he was trying not to smile. 'Well, yes. I wanted to share the good news with you the moment I found out myself.' Even as she spoke the words it was as if a double helping of conscience had reared up to mock her.

'Good to know you were thinking about me,' Alessandro commented, slanting her a look.

He didn't miss a thing, she realised edgily, moving away from the door.

'I was just around the corner in my hotel at the time,' Alessandro said, clearly trying to put her at her ease. 'What about Lech? Are you packed?'

'I haven't booked a seat yet.'

'Booked a seat?'

It took a whole new mind-set to deal with Alessandro, Emily reminded herself. Of course he would have flown to England in his own jet. 'You came for me?' she said hesitantly.

'Looks like it,' he agreed dryly.

'Can you give me half an hour? Here—let me take that for you,' she said as he began to shrug off his overcoat. 'Can I get you anything while you wait? A drink?'

'Just get ready,' he said. 'I'll wait.'

'Wait out here, then,' she suggested, opening the window to the balcony. 'It's got a fabulous view, and—'

He caught her to him as she went past, dragging her close and shutting her up with a long, deep kiss that wiped her mind clean of everything but him. But even as she softened against him he gently but very firmly pushed her away.

'Go,' he whispered. 'We have a non-negotiable take-off slot. It's nearly Christmas—or had you forgotten?'

Alessandro took her through a sumptuous wood-panelled entrance hall into a quaint reception area decorated in typical Austrian alpine style, with red gingham curtains edged with heavy ecru lace. Garlands of dried flowers hung on the walls, and in a huge stone grate a roaring log fire acted like a magnet to the people clustered around, exchanging tall stories from their day on the slopes.

There wasn't a photographer in sight, Emily noticed with relief as she watched her husband complete the formalities and return to her side with a huge old-fashioned carved wooden key-fob.

'When we get to the room I suggest you take a bath,' he said as they strolled through the hotel to the guests' accommodation. 'It's too late to sort out skis for you tonight, and mine are already here. So we'll take it easy—have dinner, chat…'

Chat. Emily nodded and smiled, but her insides were churning. There would be no more running away from the truth now. But at least he was giving her time to prepare.

As he propelled her into the lift Alessandro's hands were around her waist. His touch was electrifying. And suddenly all Emily knew, all she could think of, was that she wanted him…

'Are we going to eat in the restaurant or our room?' she asked as he pressed the button for their floor.

As an attempt to kick-start the logical side of her brain it was a pretty pathetic gambit—and she knew it—but with Alessandro so close, and no one else around, it was all she could manage.

'Why, Principessa,' he murmured softly, letting his hands slip down slowly over her thighs as the lift began to rise, 'are you hoping to seduce me?'

Resisting the temptation to lean back into him, Emily made a soft, double-barrelled sound of denial. And when he moved to drag her close she turned to face him, warning him off with her eyes. 'We have things to discuss,' she said, realising uncomfortably that he didn't know the half of it.

'Of course,' he agreed, with a small mocking bow.

But she could see the dark, smouldering desire in his eyes and the arrogant twist to his lips that proved he was remembering other occasions when the secrets between them had lain dormant and could not douse their passion.

She was relieved when the lift slowed at their floor. The atmosphere in the confined space had grown so thick with sexual tension she could feel herself drowning in it—and losing all sense of what she had come to do…to say to him. But when he stopped outside one of the heavy oak doors he rested his hand on the wall, trapping her.

'We have to share, I'm afraid. I could only get one suite because—'

'It's Christmas?' she supplied crisply, channelling all her apprehension into one snippy remark.

But he wouldn't be provoked, only stared at her lazily, forcing Emily to wonder how long she could remain immune to his unique scent…sandalwood, musk…man. And his slow smile was producing a sensory overload that made her want to drag him into the room and to hell with everything else.

But if he was in the mood for playing games… 'As we still have issues to resolve, I hope there's more than one bed in the suite?'

'Didn't I just say we'd have to share?'

'A suite…you said we had to share a suite. You didn't say anything about sharing a bed.' How come that had come out in a provocative murmur, sparing him the scolding she had intended?

'Why shouldn't we share a bed? After all, we are man and wife.'

'I hope for your sake the sofa's comfy,' Emily said, fighting to keep her voice steady as she took the key from his hand.

Just as she had feared, when she opened the door one large bed dominated the room. Spying her luggage in one corner, she hurried over to it and picked up the smallest bag. 'See you after my bath, Alessandro—'

The heel of his hand shot out, slamming into the bathroom door as she tried to close it.

'Perhaps I'd better warn you—these doors don't lock.'

'I'm sure I can trust you to be a gentleman.' Their faces were so close she could have kissed him. But, giving the door one final push, she almost sank to her knees with relief when Alessandro allowed it to close.

Inside the privacy of the marble-clad bathroom, Emily let out a long, shaky breath. With every hour that passed it became harder to tell Alessandro about the baby. She stabbed a furious glance at herself in the mirrored wall. Just when had she become such a coward? If she couldn't face up to it by the time she'd had her bath she didn't have anything to offer him—or their unborn child. It would be better for all of them if she took the next flight out of Austria...

Dinner was conducted with every outward show of restraint, whilst inwardly fires raged inside the two people facing each other across the cosy country-style table.

There was nothing remotely cosy about the workings of Emily's mind as she forked up the last scrap of home-made *sachertorte*, but she managed to hide her angst behind enthusiasm for the food.

'I've never tasted a better chocolate cake in all my life,' she said, as if they were two friends on a casual outing. 'If I stayed here for long I'd be huge.'

'You have put on a little weight,' Alessandro commented, slanting her a look as he laid down his own fork with his own cake half-eaten. And she looked better for it, he thought. She looked like some luscious fruit that was ripe and ready for eating. He swiped the linen napkin across his lips to hide his smile at his mind's meanderings. 'Not that it's a bad thing— in my opinion the extra weight suits you.'

Emily remained silent. She hadn't noticed any changes to her body—not yet. She hadn't weighed herself for a while, but…'

'Have you finished?' Alessandro said, easing his position on the carved wooden chair. 'I thought we'd have coffee sent up to the room. That way we can talk in private.'

'Fine,' Emily said quickly. She wanted to confide in him— tell him everything—and this was the best opportunity there'd been. She was already moving to her feet before Alessandro realised she meant to go right away.

'OK, OK,' he said with amusement, reaching the door a pace in front of her to open it. 'I get the message.'

Emily turned to him as they stepped into the lift. 'Do you, Alessandro?'

'I think so.'

And this time when he dragged her close she hadn't the will to resist.

Binding her hands around his neck, Emily dragged him to her with a harsh, unguarded sound of need, opening her mouth against his lips, begging for possession.

His kisses weren't enough. But as her hands flew to the buckle on his belt he dragged them away. Ramming her into the corner of the lift, he kept her wedged there while he reached across to push the lever that would stop the anti-quated contraption between floors. Then, wrenching up her slither of a skirt with one hand, he tugged off her tiny lace thong with the other.

Swinging her up, he wrapped her legs around his waist and, supporting her buttocks in hands grown firm and demanding, he entered her in one thrusting stroke, pausing only to utter a contented groan as the moist heat of her body enveloped him completely. Then, pounding into her, he answered her calls for more, increasing speed and force until she let out a long, grateful, wavering cry as the violent spasms engulfed her in sensation.

'And that's just the appetiser,' he murmured, nuzzling his face into her hair as he lowered her to the ground. 'Now get dressed,' he added sternly, bending to scoop up her discarded clothing. 'It wouldn't do for the Princess of Ferara to be seen without her knickers.'

This wasn't quite how she had pictured their first confrontation, Emily realised. But it wasn't easy to resist, when Alessandro could make her laugh at the most inappropriate moments…make her feel happy, and safe, and desired.

He hit the start lever while she struggled into her clothes. And when they reached their sumptuous suite, he slammed the door shut behind them with one hand and dragged her against him roughly with the other.

'One bed OK for you now?' he demanded huskily.

'Bed, floor, lift…' Emily breathed seductively against his mouth. 'It's all the same to me, *mi amor*.'

As he backed her towards the fluffy cream sheepskin rug in front of the roaring log fire she almost forgot what had driven her from the restaurant at such speed. But, sensing her minute mood-shift, Alessandro drew to a halt in the middle of the room.

'Coffee? Talk? Or…?'

Or would be nice, Emily thought, wavering a little, still reeling from the aftershocks of his attentions in the lift. But her rational mind insisted they couldn't go on like this. She had to tell him…tell him now.

'Coffee, please,' she managed.

'Sure?'

'No. Yes. I—'

'Coffee it is,' Alessandro said, as if nothing untoward had occurred between them since leaving the restaurant.

Releasing her to switch on some subdued lighting, he poured out two cups from the coffee tray that had been left for them some time during their extended journey between floors.

How to begin? Emily wondered, murmuring thanks as she took the cup and saucer from him.

'So. What do you want to do about these baby issues? The contract?' he prompted. 'I presume that's what all this is about?'

Emily sank down onto a small leather sofa to one side of the inglenook fireplace, stunned into silence by his remark. There were no *baby issues*. There was only a small and very vulnerable child, growing a little more inside her each day.

CHAPTER ELEVEN

THE phrase *baby issues* would not have offended her so deeply had she not been pregnant with Alessandro's baby, Emily realised. Impending motherhood had already imbued her with an overwhelming desire to protect their unborn child from everything—even the most innocent remark. And she was sure Alessandro's remark was innocent. It hadn't taken her long to discover that pregnancy hormones equalled emotional incontinence, and right now she didn't trust herself to speak in case something irrational and angry burst from her mouth.

'Well, if you won't speak to me,' he said, butting into her thoughts, 'I don't know what else I can say.' Throwing up his hands in frustration, he crossed to the window, where he stood staring out at the ghostly shadow of the snow-capped mountain that loomed like a sentinel over the village at night.

And now he was angry—and her silence was to blame, Emily realised, sensing tension so thick in the air it hung like smog, keeping each of them isolated in their own lonely space. But how could she discuss their baby as if it was nothing more than a clause in a contract? She stared in dismay at the huge double bed that only seemed to mock her desire to resume normal relations with her husband.

'Alessandro—'

He turned and looked at her, his head slightly dipped and

a furrow of concentration scoring a deep line between his eyes.

It was as if his vision cleared and he had time to study his wife properly for the first time in weeks, Alessandro realised. She looked so weary—exhausted, he amended. Why hadn't he noticed that before?

'Don't be angry,' Emily said softly. 'I really need to be with you tonight.'

His head jerked in surprised response, but he hid his feelings quickly. How had it come to this?

'Where else would you be?' he said gently, reaching out his hands. And when she took them he drew her into his arms.

He held her in his arms all night, dressed in the bizarre outfit it turned out was all she had brought with her—a long baggy tee shirt, with the logo showing only faintly on the front after too many washes, and a pair of stripy pyjama bottoms that trailed over her feet.

He had made no comment when she came out of the bathroom after her shower. And said nothing more when she climbed into the high, comfortable four-poster-bed and pulled the sheets up to her chin. He just climbed in after her, wearing a pair of boxer shorts for the sake of decency, rolled onto his back, and switched out the light.

He wasn't sure exactly when she edged towards him, only that she had…and he stroked the hair back from her brow and kissed her while she was sleeping, as she whimpered in his arms from some deep-seated despair.

He must have dropped off some time during the night, because he woke to find her at the window, staring out, peering from side to side as if there was something quite extraordinary happening outside.

Turning, as if she felt his waking presence as keenly as if he had spoken, she said,

'Alessandro, I think we're snowed in.'

Emily waited as he stretched and yawned noisily, then sat

up and raked through his wayward black hair in a hopeless attempt to tame it.

Padding across the room to join her, he leaned his fists on the windowsill and gazed out across what had become in a few short hours a featureless snowscape.

'No chance of anyone leaving Lech today,' he murmured.

Where there had been pavements and cars and railings, marking the banks of the river that wound its way through the village, there was only a uniform blanket of deep white snow.

'Hungry?' he said, not appearing too concerned by this turn of events.

'A little,' Emily admitted, trying to ignore the fact that her husband was naked, apart from his hip-skimming boxer shorts, and standing very close.

'I'll ring down—have them send something up to us. I feel lazy today. We might as well take it easy…after all, we're not going anywhere.'

Emily moved away to put on some more logs and stoke the dying embers of the fire. The fact that they had slept in the same bed together and he hadn't attempted to make love to her had left her feeling restless and uneasy. Was he still angry with her? Maybe he didn't want her any more. Maybe he was going to reinstate the celibacy clause in their agreement. Maybe he would find that all too easy.

'How long do you think we're here for?' she said, pulling herself together, knowing she sounded edgy, as if she didn't want to be snowed in with him, when nothing could be further from the truth.

But Alessandro seemed not to notice. He had the phone in his hand and was gesturing for her to wait as he got through to Room Service. He spoke rapidly in German…something else she hadn't known about her husband, she realised, feeling panic sweep over her. The fact was, she didn't know much about him at all.

'That's settled,' he said, replacing the receiver. 'Relax,

Emily. There's nothing we can do. We might just as well settle back and enjoy the break. Why don't you stop prowling around the room? Go and have a nice long soak in the bath while we're waiting for breakfast to arrive.'

Did he want to put distance between them? Emily swallowed down the fear that had lodged in her throat. All her emotions seemed to be in turmoil—all the time; every little thing seemed to assume crisis proportions. 'How long?' she said again.

'Breakfast? Or—?'

'No, not breakfast,' she flashed back. 'You know what I'm talking about, Alessandro.'

'Do I, Emily?' he said. 'I know you're very prickly this morning, and over-sensitive. Is it something I've done—or not done?'

Her face flamed as the thought of what he had not done. And when she saw the faintly ironic shadow in his slanting amber gaze she knew for sure he was reading her mind.

'You seem to be in a great hurry to leave Lech,' he pressed. 'Do you have an urgent appointment to keep elsewhere?'

'No, of course not.' Emily's mind lurched back on track. 'I came here to be with you—to thank you properly for helping me with that case.'

Is that all? Alessandro thought as he snatched up his robe. Thrusting his arms into the sleeves, he threw her a cynical look. So, Emily only wanted to thank him for his help with her case? It was almost worse than being told she had only come for the sex. 'To answer to your question,' he said coolly, securing the belt, 'walking parties may be able to leave here quite soon with a local guide. Others, who are not quite so desperate to return to reality, can stay on at the hotel until the road down to Zurs is cleared.'

'Oh…' Emily said, peering distractedly out of the window.

'Which category of snowbound guest do you fall into, Emily?'

She moved back towards the fireplace, where the logs were well ablaze. 'I'm staying,' she said without hesitation.

'And we'll do what?'

Now it was Alessandro's turn to sound as if he was having difficulty reining in his feelings—as if he was determined that the emotional rollercoaster ride she had subjected him to had made its final run. It was time to build bridges between them, Emily realised, before the moment was lost for ever...

'I don't know,' she said, determined to find something that would bring them close again. 'Tell each other stories?'

His gaze narrowed thoughtfully, and then, to her relief, softened a little.

'For instance?'

'How about the one you never finished...the one about this ring,' she suggested, holding out her hand so that the central stone in the beautiful old piece of jewellery glowed like a drop of crimson blood in the firelight.

Their relationship was like a ball of wool that had become hopelessly tangled, Emily thought as he came to sit down on the sofa while she chose a spot on the rug. Telling each other stories wouldn't have been her first choice for Christmas Eve activities, but it was somewhere to start teasing out the knots.

'You reached the point where Caterina found the ring and believed it was a sign from Rodrigo,' she prompted.

'OK,' Alessandro said, settling back. 'So Caterina was forced to accept that her lover had drowned. But she decided she couldn't lock herself away in a religious community after all, and would live her life as Rodrigo would have wanted her to.'

'How could she know what he wanted?'

'Because that was the moment she realised she was pregnant with his child.'

Emily's glance flashed up, but there was no separate agenda, she saw thankfully—he was only recounting a much-loved story.

'Caterina put Rodrigo's ring on her finger and returned to Ferara to fulfil her destiny. And every Princess of Ferara has worn the ring you have on your finger since that day.'

'That's the most romantic thing I ever heard,' Emily admitted, turning the ring around her finger so that the flames from the fire seemed to imbue it with life…or with challenge, maybe… And now it was her turn to come up with an equivalent tale. How would she begin? *Alessandro, I'm going to tell you the story of a baby*?

'I'm sure the history of that ring has been embellished over the years until it's little more than a fairytale,' Alessandro said, misreading the questions in her mind. 'Emily? Where are you going?'

'To have that bath you suggested.' To give herself time.

'You don't get out of telling your story that easily,' Alessandro warned. 'I'll order breakfast while you're reclining in bubbles, then it's your turn.'

Putting a CD on to play, Emily slipped the slim volume of poetry Alessandro had given to her, with the Christopher Marlowe rose from her wedding bouquet pressed inside it, between his jeans and jumper, where he was sure to find it, before heading for the bathroom.

'What are you doing?' he said suspiciously as she darted about the room.

'Nothing.'

'This music—?'

Her shoulders dropped with relief that the first part of her plan hadn't failed. 'Miranda's first commercial recording.'

'It's quite remarkable,' Alessandro murmured, remaining very still as he listened.

'It was brought out in time for Christmas. This is the first copy off the press. Miranda wanted you to have it…she signed it for you.' Hurrying to his side, Emily pressed the empty case into his hands. 'I suppose I should have wrapped it up—'

'No, this is perfect,' Alessandro insisted. And before she could get away he caught hold of her hands and raised them to his lips. 'Go and have your bath, Emily—and don't be long.'

The message in his eyes was unmistakable...irresistible. Emily held his gaze. Her heart was thundering in her chest. It was going to be all right. Everything was going to be all right...

'Do I have to?' she protested after her bath, when they were both sitting by the fire again. 'I'm fine with facts, but I'm absolutely hopeless at telling stories.'

'Then if you can't play the game,' Alessandro warned, 'you'll have to pay a forfeit.'

There was only a glint of humour in his eyes, but it was enough for Emily to feel as if the whole world had revolved on its axis and returned them to a moment in time before secrets had driven a wedge between them. 'A forfeit?'

'Certainly,' he murmured, in a voice that hovered between stern and seductive. Reaching towards her, he brushed a wayward strand of hair back from her face with one finger. 'And I get to choose what that forfeit should be.'

Emily's nerves were jangling with awareness.

She was acutely conscious of the crackling of the logs in the grate and the barely discernible patter of snow against the window as his hand moved to cup the back of her head and draw her close. As his warm, musky man-scent invaded the clean air she made no move to resist when he gathered her into his arms.

'Thank you for the rose,' he whispered against her lips, and even though his eyes were half closed Emily could see how bright they flared with passion, and with love.

'And for the gift of music. I can't think of a better Christmas present.'

'Except this,' she murmured seductively, drawing him down with her onto the soft rug in front of the fire. It felt like a homecoming, a long awaited return. She was lost from the moment his lips touched her body. And when his tongue began to work on her nipples there was no possibility of turning back.

Moving lower, Alessandro freed the fastenings on her jeans and took them down, together the tiny thong she was wearing. Naked now, Emily moved sinuously beneath him as he covered her waist and her belly with tiny teasing bites, before moving on to the insides of her thighs. Running her hands appreciatively over his back, she felt bereft when he left her briefly to tug off his clothes.

There was nothing wrong in having your husband make love to you, Emily reassured herself when something dark and unfathomable niggled at the back of her mind—nothing but the knowledge that you were really four months pregnant with his child and he didn't know yet! She pulled away as his kisses grew a lot more intimate.

'What?' he said, but there was already a hard look in his eyes—as if he knew, Emily saw apprehensively. But how could he know? 'You taste different.'

She was so thrown by the comment that it took her a few moments to rally her thoughts. 'Different?' she muttered.

'You heard what I said.'

The change in Alessandro's voice, in his mood, was frightening. Backing away, Emily sat up and hugged her knees to her chest. 'How do you mean, different?'

His eyes had narrowed and his gaze was calculating. 'I can't list the contributory factors like a recipe—'

'The *contributory factors*?' Emily demanded, reaching nervously for her clothes. 'Don't ever accuse *me* of lawyer-speak again!' Her attempt to lighten the mood skittered across the frigid silence between them, making no improvement. Stumbling awkwardly around, she pulled on her clothes. 'I should never have come,' she exclaimed when Alessandro made no response. 'I'm going to call down to Reception and find out when that guide will be leaving the village—'

'Put that down!'

One minute he was on the rug gazing up at her; the next he was standing beside her with the telephone in his hand.

'I think you owe me an explanation, Emily.'

'No—why—?' she said, backing away from the look in his eyes.

'I think you know. How many months pregnant are you, Emily? Why didn't you tell me the moment you found out?'

Emily's head spun and the ground seemed to come up to meet her. This was the very last thing she had wanted. The hurt in his voice jabbed at her mind like so many thorns.

'How long were you prepared to wait before you told me?'

'Stop!' She put her hands over her ears, as if she couldn't bear to hear another word. 'Please, Alessandro, stop firing questions at me. I can't think—'

'That's perfectly obvious.'

She glanced at him, then quickly looked away. Everything that had been between them minutes earlier had been replaced by an expression on his face that chilled her to the marrow. 'I'm sorry—'

'You set a great scene; I'll hand you that,' he said bitterly, swiping one angry hand across the back of his neck.'

'A scene? What do you mean?'

'The music, the poetry, the rose,' he flashed accusingly. 'I would have preferred honesty…and from the start. Why couldn't you just trust me?'

Silence swooped down between them, holding them apart, until finally Alessandro said in a voice so low she could hardly be sure he spoke at all, 'It's my fault. That damnable clause in our country's constitution—I should have told you—'

'Stop it!' Her cry rang harshly round them after his murmured confession. 'I'm at fault, too, Alessandro,' Emily insisted desperately. 'But I was frightened—'

'Frightened?' He looked stunned. Wheeling away from her, he raked stiff fingers through his hair, and then stopped again, as if he hardly knew what he was doing. 'I can't stand this,' he admitted, shaking his head distractedly. 'I can't bear what's happening between us—and most of all I can't bear to think you were frightened of me.'

'I was never frightened of you,' Emily admitted softly. 'I was frightened of losing you…frightened of what it will mean to all of us…you, me, and especially our child…when that wretched contract comes to an end.'

'Contract!' He made a sound of disgust as he turned his face away. 'I should never have put my name to it in the first place.'

'We both entered into it in good faith,' Emily pointed out. 'We just didn't expect to have feelings get in the way of a business deal.'

'Can you ever forgive me?' he demanded tensely, staring at her as if his very life depended on her answer.

'Easily,' Emily said as she touched his arm. 'We've both made mistakes. Neither of us was prepared for how our feelings would grow. That contract was drawn up to satisfy our business instincts, not our emotions. I know I should never have left you…but when I found out about the clause in the constitution that demanded an heir before your father could abdicate I couldn't think straight—'

'And no wonder,' Alessandro admitted, very slowly drawing her into his arms, as if he needed to be certain she knew that was where she belonged. 'And now?'

'Now?'

'Can you think straight now?' he demanded softly.

'I hope so…I don't know.' She shrugged with exasperation. 'I'm just so—'

'Pregnant?' he supplied gently, a wry smile playing around his lips as he looked at her. 'This is the first time for you and the first time for me…and I am totally overwhelmed to know we are expecting a child. Your hormones must be in turmoil. Don't be so hard on yourself, Emily.'

As he dipped his head to kiss her Emily made herself pull back. 'Are you quite sure that marriage to a commoner is what you really want, Alessandro?'

'What on earth do you mean?' He drew his head back to stare at her in bemusement. 'How can you even ask me a question like that?'

'There must be so many women of noble birth who would jump at the chance—'

'And none of them is you.'

'But it can't have been easy for your father when you told him.'

Alessandro placed his finger over her lips. 'My father loves you, Emily.'

'You can trace your ancestors back thirty generations—'

'And half of them were warlords,' Alessandro broke in firmly. 'Brigands who snatched power from those weaker than themselves. They would be considered beyond the pale in today's society.'

'But still—'

'No, Emily,' he said firmly. 'Stop this right now. Did you know that Christopher Marlowe was the son of a shoemaker? No?' he said, staring at her intently. 'And yet he was a far greater prince than I. We quote his words more than four hundred years after his death. Who will remember my words?'

'You share your father's passion for Tudor playwrights,' Emily exclaimed, her face breaking into a smile as she relaxed at last.

'It would be impossible to live under the same roof as my father and not share his passions,' Alessandro admitted wryly. 'And one of his most profound, my love, is you.'

'And yet I've been so unreasonable—to both of you.'

'No,' Alessandro argued gently. 'You're a woman in love,

a pregnant woman in love, and with a man you're still getting to know.'

'So, where do we go from here?' she said anxiously, scanning his face.

'That's the easy part,' he murmured, kissing her again.

When Alessandro insisted they should both dress for dinner that evening Emily didn't have the heart to refuse him, even though she expected the small, exclusive hotel festivities to be low-key.

The floor-length gown, packed into her suitcase at the last minute in a moment of whimsy, was of crimson silk, and emphasised the creamy whiteness of her skin. She felt particularly comfortable in it because it draped elegantly over her fuller figure. Leaving her hair to fall loosely around her shoulders, she wore the minimum of make-up—just some lip-gloss and soft grey eyeshadow to point up the brilliant jade-green of her eyes.

Wondering what Alessandro had planned, she found herself ready before him, and had to keep reminding herself that this was the man who loved her while she watched with naked appreciation as he dressed after his shower.

As he slipped into his dinner jacket, and made final adjustments to his hair in the mirror, he smiled back at her. 'I think it's time for your Christmas present,' he said, shooting her the type of look that always made her melt.

'But we've just got dressed—' She stopped at his amused glance of male awareness. The sound of his voice was enough to arouse her, she realised self-consciously. But he instead of moving towards her he made for the door. 'Alessandro?' Emily called after him anxiously. 'Where are you going?'

'I said it was time for your Christmas present now,' he reminded her. Removing what looked like a single sheet of paper from his jacket pocket, he left it on the oak dresser by the door. 'While I'm gone, you might like to cast your eyes over this,' he suggested. And then, before she had a chance to say a word, he left the room.

'Alessandro, wait—' Emily's heart gave a sickening lurch as she rushed towards the door. Swinging it open, she stared both ways down the corridor. But everything was silent. He was nowhere to be seen. Coming back into the room, she closed the door behind her. Biting her lip, she snatched up the sheet of paper and began to read.

Alessandro's bold pen-work leaped off the page at her, his blue ink resonating purposefully against the thick ivory-coloured sheet.

> *'Come live with me, and be my Love,*
> *And we will all the pleasures prove…*
> *If these delights thy mind may move! Then live with*
> *me, and be my Love.*

Two minds with but a single thought… When would she ever learn to trust him?

'Alessandro—' She whirled round as he came back into the room. 'I read the poem.'

'Did you like it?'

The confidence in his eyes thrilled her. 'Of course.' She wondered if they would ever make it down for dinner…

'So, I chose well?'

'How can you ask?'

'I apologise for leaving you so abruptly,' he said, crossing to her side. 'I just wanted to check everything was ready.'

'Ready?' The restaurant table, she surmised, imagining how busy the hotel would be on Christmas Eve.

'Yes. We have to go out onto the balcony.'

'The balcony?'

'Do you have a wrap? Here, take this.'

Before she could stop him, Alessandro had shrugged off his own jacket and was wrapping it around her shoulders.

'You'll freeze,' Emily said, looking at him with concern. 'And why the balcony?'

'Stop asking questions,' Alessandro said, snatching up another jacket from the chair. 'We'll miss everything.'

'What?'

But Alessandro was in no mood for conversation as he hurried her outside.

The balcony overlooking the immense, mountain peaks in front of them was beautifully lit, and there were heaters, strategically placed by the hotel, so that instead of feeling cold, as she had expected to, Emily felt positively cosy as she sank into the comforting warmth of Alessandro's jacket.

The particular balcony on which they were standing went right around the hotel, and more people were joining them, Emily noticed, trickling out of their rooms in twos and—

'Mum? Dad!' she gasped, seeing who it was. Bolting towards them, she gave them each a hug, laughing with surprise. Then, at her father's gentle prompting, she turned. 'Your Royal Highness—' Turning to Alessandro, she could only shake her head in speechless delight.

'Happy Christmas, my darling,' he whispered, drawing her close to plant a tender kiss on her lips. 'Look—' he said, including everyone as he gestured towards the mountain. 'They're about to start.'

'What…what's happening?' Emily demanded softly, looking for answers to Alessandro.

'Watch the top of the mountain,' Alessandro instructed, holding her in front of him as everyone else gathered round.

At first all Emily could see was a cluster of light, right at the top of the tallest peak. 'Where's Miranda?' she whispered, as her mother came to stand next to her at the front rail of the balcony.

'Listen,' Alessandro commanded, silencing everyone.

As she waited, Emily noticed that the whole village seemed to be out on the streets; people were standing on the wall by the river and on the parapet of the bridge to get a better look. But the silence was absolute as they all stood staring at the top of the mountain.

Emily jumped closer to Alessandro when she heard a cannon being fired, somewhere far away. The loud report echoed several times, fading with each repetition as the shots bounced off each majestic rockface in turn. As it fell completely silent again a haunting melody shimmered through the crisp mountain air.

'Miranda!' Her sister's playing was uniquely beautiful and Emily would have known it anywhere. Alessandro's hold around her waist tightened a little as he burrowed his face into her neck to give her a kiss of confirmation.

The limpid sound of the solo violin was completely suited to the magical occasion, and as the sound rose through the speakers judicially placed throughout the village a murmur arose from the crowds on the streets, and then applause.

As Alessandro pointed up towards the jagged peak again Emily could see that the tiny cluster of light at the top of the mountain had split up to form a chain, and was now beginning to stream down the slopes in a long, curling ribbon of light.

'The ski instructors—each holding a torch,' Alessandro explained, and the shimmering line took its cue from the waltz Miranda was playing and swung in giant rhythmical loops across the mountainside as they came down towards the village.

'It's magical!' Emily murmured, leaning back into Alessandro. 'The best…the very best Christmas present I could ever have.'

'Don't speak too soon,' Alessandro murmured close to her ear, so that her whole body ached for him.

After the display they ate a light meal together. Miranda joined them, flushed and happy with success, and accompanied by a rather striking-looking man who, Emily learned, having won a gold medal in the downhill ski race at the Winter Olympics, had been granted the honour of leading the torchlight procession of skiers down the mountain.

When they had finished eating Alessandro led everyone back onto the balcony, to see a barrage of fireworks screaming into the night sky, illuminating the inky blackness with endless plumes of exploding light.

'Happy Christmas, *belissima*,' he murmured, as every clock in the village struck midnight.

'Happy Christmas, Alessandro,' Emily whispered in return, wondering if anyone in the world had ever been as happy as she was.

'Alessandro! Emily!'

Releasing their hold on each other, they turned to share their happiness with Alessandro's father.

'Tonight you have made an old man very happy,' he said, opening his arms wide to embrace them both. 'This—this is what I have wished for since our first meeting in the garden,' he added, turning to address Emily. 'I would gladly cede all the privileges life has granted me to see my son Alessandro as happy as he is now—with you, Emily. And to know,' he added archly, 'that for the very first time in his life he has met his match.'

Was that a wink? Emily wondered, laughing back. She was so happy. 'I will do my best to keep things that way,' she promised, matching his conspiratorial tone.

'I know you will,' the elderly Prince declared confidently. 'And as for you, Alessandro—' He turned to face his son. 'You are a very lucky man. And now…' He turned around to draw Emily's family into the conversation. 'I think it's time we left these two lovebirds alone. I would be honoured if you would all join me in my suite for a nightcap before we retire to bed.'

Giving her mother and father a warm kiss each, Emily saved a special hug for Miranda, taking the chance to murmur, 'I like him,' when she sensed Miranda's handsome new conquest was uppermost in her twin's mind. Embracing Alessandro's father, she kissed him on both cheeks and whispered, 'Thank you for everything…and thank you especially for Alessandro.'

With a last squeeze, he released her back into the arms of her husband.

'Goodnight to you both, and a happy Christmas to everyone.' With one last expansive gesture he led Emily's family away.

Under protection of the darkness Alessandro's lips brushed lightly against Emily's neck, and then moved on to her cheek, her mouth, always light, almost testing—as if they were on a first date. The thought excited her, and she turned her face up to him to whisper, 'Don't stop.'

'You're very forward, Principessa,' he growled softly. 'Do you think we had better go inside?'

Emily's limbs felt as if they had turned into molten honey as he swept her into his arms and carried her back into their suite.

Glimpsing her reflection in the mirror at the side of the bed, she watched Alessandro release the hooks on the back of her dress. As his hands moved lower he began to kiss the back of her neck and her shoulders, until she was leaning into him, sighing with pleasure. The jewelled pins in her hair made it seem scattered with stars, and he released them so that the ebony waves tumbled over her shoulders. Her breasts were creamy against the crimson silk bodice, the shadow of her cleavage deep and dark—

'Stop looking in the mirror,' he murmured. 'I want all your attention on me.'

'That's not so hard,' Emily admitted softly as the dress fell away and he eased it over her hips.

'Beautiful,' he murmured, looking at her admiringly as his hands moved to cup her breasts. 'I should like to keep you here for ever.'

'I should have to leave the bedroom some time,' Emily teased, but she gasped as his thumb-pads stroked firmly against her nipples.

'Don't worry, I would never stop my wife doing the job she loves,' he insisted, his gold eyes darkening to sepia as he observed her arousal. 'But not tonight,' he continued softly, sternly. 'I have never wished to narrow your horizons, Emily…only to broaden them.' And then, allowing her to sink back onto the soft pillows, he stood up and pulled off his clothes.

She was definitely ready to have her horizons broadened again, Emily thought, watching him strip. A familiar lethargy was already invading her limbs, and before he even touched her shafts of sensation were streaming through her body. As he lay down beside her she feared she was about to discover if it was possible to climax from anticipation alone.

Coming closer, he caressed her ear with his lips, moving on to nibble the tender lobe. And all the while his warm breath fanned her pulse, making her long for the firmer touch of his hands, a touch he knew just how long to deny her. Then his weight was controlling her, his hands positioning her, until she could do no more than submit—a licence he made full use of until she lay calm and sated in his arms once again.

And later, much later, when Alessandro was tracing the gently curving swell of her belly with awe, he murmured, 'No more separation for us, Emily—ever. When you have a case in London we will move Court over there, so that I can be with you…the baby, too, of course,' he said, a smile coming to his face as he looked at her. 'We will buy a suitable property. I don't see a problem.'

'I'm sure you don't,' Emily said, smiling as she ran her nail-tips gently through his tousled hair, making him gasp aloud with pleasure at her touch. 'But when have you ever seen a problem that you couldn't solve, Alessandro? I don't believe a problem ever existed that could defeat you.'

'I almost met my match with you, Emily,' he admitted wryly. 'That is, of course, until I found the perfect way of dealing with you…'

She sucked in a swift breath as he entered her again, smoothly and firmly, filling her completely.

'I can't argue—' She couldn't speak. Pleasure had stolen her words away. And then his lips and tongue claimed her mouth, finally completing the task.

Could there be more happiness in all the world than this? Emily wondered late on Christmas morning, when Alessandro swung out of bed and left her briefly.

'Another Christmas present,' he explained, coming back to her side. 'And this time it's for both of us.'

'What is it?' she said excitedly.

'This,' Alessandro said, as he held out an official-looking document.

When she went to take it from him he only shook his head, and then, very slowly and deliberately, began to tear it into tiny pieces.

'What are you doing?' she asked in surprise.

'Something I should have done months ago. That is what I think of our contract.' Turning around, he dropped the tiny scraps of paper into the wastebin by the side of the bed. 'Now it can never come between us again,' he said, coming back to stretch out beside her. Drawing her into his arms, he murmured, 'I love you, Emily—my wife, my only love, mother of my child—my children,' he corrected himself with a long, lazy smile.'

'And I love you, too, Alessandro,' Emily said as she wrapped her arms around him and snuggled into his chest. 'With all my heart.'

'So,' he murmured slumberously, 'will you live with me and be my love, Emily?'

'I will,' she whispered, taking hold of his hand and placing it against her belly to feel their baby's first forceful kicks.

Virgin Brides, Arrogant Husbands

Demure but defiant...
Can three international playboys
tame their disobedient brides?

Proud, masculine and passionate, these men
are used to having it all. But enter Ophelia,
Abbey and Molly, three feisty virgins to whom
their wealth and power mean little. In stories
filled with drama, desire and secrets of the
past, find out how these arrogant husbands
capture their hearts....

Available in December

THE GREEK TYCOON'S
DISOBEDIENT BRIDE
#2779

THE Sheikh Tycoons

by *Sandra Marton*

*They're powerful, passionate—
and as sexy as sin!*

Three desert princes—
how will they tame their feisty brides?

Sheikh Salim al Taj has unfinished business with
Grace, his errant mistress. When they get stranded
on an exotic island, things really heat up!

This miniseries concludes with

THE SHEIKH'S
REBELLIOUS MISTRESS

Book #2782

Available December

REQUEST YOUR FREE BOOKS!

 HARLEQUIN *Presents* ®

2 FREE NOVELS PLUS 2 FREE GIFTS!

YES! Please send me 2 FREE Harlequin Presents® novels and my 2 FREE gifts (gifts are worth about $10). After receiving them, if I don't wish to receive any more books, I can return the shipping statement marked "cancel". If I don't cancel, I will receive 6 brand-new novels every month and be billed just $4.05 per book in the U.S. or $4.74 per book in Canada, plus 25¢ shipping and handling per book and applicable taxes, if any*. That's a savings of close to 15% off the cover price! I understand that accepting the 2 free books and gifts places me under no obligation to buy anything. I can always return a shipment and cancel at any time. Even if I never buy another book, the two free books and gifts are mine to keep forever.

106 HDN ERRW   306 HDN ERRL

Name _____ (PLEASE PRINT) _____

Address _____ Apt. # _____

City _____ State/Prov. _____ Zip/Postal Code _____

Signature (if under 18, a parent or guardian must sign)

Mail to the **Harlequin Reader Service:**
IN U.S.A.: P.O. Box 1867, Buffalo, NY 14240-1867
IN CANADA: P.O. Box 609, Fort Erie, Ontario L2A 5X3

Not valid to current subscribers of Harlequin Presents books.

Want to try two free books from another line?
Call 1-800-873-8635 or visit www.morefreebooks.com.

* Terms and prices subject to change without notice. N.Y. residents add applicable sales tax. Canadian residents will be charged applicable provincial taxes and GST. Offer not valid in Quebec. This offer is limited to one order per household. All orders subject to approval. Credit or debit balances in a customer's account(s) may be offset by any other outstanding balance owed by or to the customer. Please allow 4 to 6 weeks for delivery. Offer available while quantities last.

Your Privacy: Harlequin Books is committed to protecting your privacy. Our Privacy Policy is available online at www.eHarlequin.com or upon request from the Reader Service. From time to time we make our lists of customers available to reputable third parties who may have a product or service of interest to you. If you would prefer we not share your name and address, please check here. ☐

HP08R

I ♥ HARLEQUIN *Presents*

BROUGHT TO YOU BY FANS OF
HARLEQUIN PRESENTS.

We are its editors and authors
and biggest fans—and we'd
love to hear from YOU!

Subscribe today to our online blog at
www.iheartpresents.com

EXTRA

THE ITALIAN'S BRIDE

Commanded—to be his wife!

Used to the finest food, clothes and women, these immensely powerful, incredibly good-looking and undeniably charismatic men have only one last need: a wife!

They've chosen their bride-to-be and they'll have her—willing or not!

Enjoy all our fantastic stories in December:

THE ITALIAN BILLIONAIRE'S SECRET LOVE-CHILD
by CATHY WILLIAMS (Book #33)

SICILIAN MILLIONAIRE, BOUGHT BRIDE
by CATHERINE SPENCER (Book #34)

BEDDED AND WEDDED FOR REVENGE
by MELANIE MILBURNE (Book #35)

THE ITALIAN'S UNWILLING WIFE
by KATHRYN ROSS (Book #36)